SOMEBODY'S FOREVER

ROBBI RENEE

Note from the Publisher: This is a work of fiction. Any resemblance to actual persons living or dead or references to locations, persons, events, or locations are purely coincidental. The characters, circumstances, and events are imaginative and not intended to reflect actual events.

BY ROBBI RENEE

Somebody's Forever
Copyright © 2023 Love Notes by Robbi Renee
All rights reserved and proprietary.

No part of this book may be reproduced in any form or format without
the written consent of the Author.
Send all requests to lovenotes@lovenotesbyrobbirenee.com

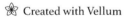 Created with Vellum

SYNOPSIS

Zeke & Jules' situationship continues in Somebody's Forever.
Will they find happily ever after, or was it fun while it lasted?
After a tumultuous divorce, Dr. Jemma Holiday simply wanted a
fresh start... with Dr. Ezekiel Green.

Living in the small college town of Monroe City, Jemma was
reluctant to go public with the new relationship. At the same time,
Ezekiel was ready to share the love for his beautiful Jules with the
world.

Jemma wanted to be somebody's girlfriend. She wanted a man she
could love with no shame. But was Jules moving too fast with the
good doctor Zeke or was this whirlwind love affair right on time?
Ezekiel wanted to be somebody's forever, to love every beautiful
flaw, every imperfection of a woman. Zeke wanted to be Jemma's
forever.

DEDICATION

My Perfect Personal Love Note
Written for Robbi Renee
by
The Husband, George L. Cleveland

I've searched the world for someone like you
Someone who makes my heart feel brand new
You're the missing piece that I've been searching for
And I'll love you forevermore.

You're my perfect love notes, my melody
The only one who truly understands me
With you, my heart is complete
You are the reason that I breathe.

You're my best friend, my confidant
You're everything a man could ever want
Together we're unstoppable, we're a team

I never want to wake up from this dream.

You're the love of my life, my ride or die
With you, I'll always feel alive
I'll cherish every moment that we share
I'll always be right there.

You're my perfect love notes, my harmony
With you, I'll always be happy
Forever and always, you're my destiny
My perfect love notes, you complete me.

1

JULES

*O*bsessed. *Jonesing. Hooked. Consistently engaging in behaviors providing immediate sensory rewards.* This was a pretty accurate description of the dependency, my uncontrollable addiction to Dr. Ezekiel Green. I'd indulged in the glory of that man for the past several weeks since we confessed our love for each other. An insatiable whirlwind defined the adventurous journey that Zeke and I had embarked on. That man had my mind, body, and soul spinning topsy-turvy. I was gluttonous, starving for him at every turn, and my hotsy-totsy ass wasn't embarrassed about it one bit.

Ezekiel had been in New York the past week checking on his mother since she'd been dealing with the aftereffects of the coronavirus. He was supposed to return last night, but his flight was canceled due to storms in St. Louis. Today was graduation at Monroe University, and I was praying that he would arrive in time to give his first commencement speech as Provost.

Dressed in my graduation regalia, I hurriedly ambled through the Ossie and Ruby Davis Theatre, giving instructions to ensure the ceremony was flawlessly delivered. I'd been checking my phone all morning but no word from Zeke.

"Jemma. Eat." Maxine demanded, shoving a banana in my direction as I ensured the chairs were correctly positioned on the stage. "You have been prancing around here like a chicken without a head. You're going to make yourself sick. He'll be here."

I audibly huffed, then nodded. Peeling the banana to take a bite, I couldn't understand why I was so nervous. I'd organized and attended countless graduation ceremonies at Monroe University, but what was so special about this one? *Him.*

Dr. Green had not only made an enormous impression on me, but he'd been extremely instrumental to the growth of the university this school year. His fundraising efforts in such a short time supported more scholarships and future infrastructure to expand the campus. Monroe was even featured in *Essence Magazine* for the mental health initiative Seen.Heard.Supported, co-chaired by Ezekiel and me. Given his accolades, I wanted him to have the opportunity to be recognized for his leadership.

Hurrying down the hall, returning to my frantic headless chicken behavior, I felt a forceful tug on my robe, pulling me backward into a room. A large hand closed the door, trapping me as I quickly turned around and was prepared to give somebody a piece of my mind when my eyes connected with familiar onyx orbs.

"Zeke," I squealed like a schoolgirl, tightly wrapping my arms around his neck.

He looked so damn good in his maroon and gold Provost regalia. The freshly groomed beard, bald head, and dark-rimmed glasses sent shockwaves through my yoni. *Goddamn, this man is fine.*

His arms encased me and felt like the softest place on earth. Lately, they'd been my peace, the only place I sought respite during moments of uncertainty. He delicately kneaded down the center of my back before his hands reached my ass.

"Mmm, baby, I missed you," Zeke muttered as he kissed along the arc of my chin before reaching my lips.

"Zee, mmm, I missed you too," I panted, clasping my hands tighter around his neck.

Caressing his bald head, I grabbed his ears to draw him nearer to me as his tongue-lashing grew more intense.

"When did you get in?" I said, moaning as he nibbled and licked my flesh.

"About forty minutes ago. I got dressed and came straight here. Nevermind the particulars, what's up under this robe?" he muttered, snaking his hands under the heavy fabric.

"Dr. Green, we only have twenty minutes before the processional begins." I lightly swatted away his hands, feigning innocence.

"Perfect timing," he said, groaning as he unzipped my robe and then his.

I wore a mustard-colored wrap dress that offered him easy access to do whatever he wanted. Ezekiel's massive hands stroked up the length of my smooth legs before reaching my apex. The seat of my thong was already drenched just from the familiarity of his natural vanilla aroma. We simultaneously gasped when he slithered a finger against the seam of my panties to gain access to my puss. Two fingers stealthily slipped down my private folds entering my essence.

"Aah, Zee," I yelped, breathing labored.

"You know this quick shit is usually not my style, but I need to be inside of you, Jemma. Right fucking now, baby," he mumbled.

"Mmm..." I croaked, incapable of forming a coherent sentence.

"Can I fuck you, Jules? Please, baby."

"Yes, Zee, please," I blurted, getting my vocabulary together real quick, granting this man full permission to devour me.

We were still at the door of the room that I now discovered was the private quarters reserved for him to get prepared for the ceremony. Zeke reached behind me to ensure the door was locked. He ushered me to the vanity in the corner. Spinning me around, my back was against his chest as we gazed at each other's reflection in the mirror. I gathered the dress around my waist and casually dipped my hips, issuing him my ass to take. He bit the corner of those luscious lips and then winked. I was all too familiar with that wink. Ezekiel, the animalistic beast, was about to be unleashed.

His pants and briefs were pooled at his feet in an instant. That magnificent artifact he called *a dick* sprang forward, ready, willing, and able to harshly invade my pussy. Although this was a quickie, Zeke entered me slowly, filling me inch by extraordinary inch by astounding inch.

"Goddamn, Jules," he roared in a low, gruff tone.

Ezekiel wrapped a firm hand around my neck while the other gripped my ass. He gently squeezed, causing me to momentarily lose my breath. His hold tightened as the pace accelerated. Our reflections connected in the mirror, and this man peered directly into my narrowed eyes with so much animalistic lust and amorous love as he choked, thrust, and pounded me.

"Shit, Jules. You got me coming already. Damn," he groaned, pummeled, and pelted.

"Zee. Oh my God. Me too, babe. Don't stop, don't st-"

His hand over my mouth captured the looming thunderous bellow.

Knock. Knock.

"Dr. Green, we'll be ready for you to line up in five minutes." The annoying voice of Christina Hall sounded from the other side of the door. "Dr. Green, are you OK?" was shouted, followed by more knocking.

"Yes. I'm good. Thank you. Five minutes," he said, grunting through gritted teeth.

Fuck her, don't stop was about to spill from my lungs when he put his finger in my mouth to silence me, but the energetic thrashing did not cease.

Zeke was so deep, my damn eyes crossed, then rolled to the back of my head. A mumbled "Mmm" escaped my lips while I sucked his fingers like it was... *him.*

There was no use in fighting it anymore. I simply closed my eyes tight and fell into the abyss of Ezekiel. My body went limp, lungs inoperable as I surrendered to the beautiful battering until we jointly reached a violent climax.

"Juulleess," he hushly roared, spilling his seeds inside of me.

Erratic, labored gasps were my only response. My body buckled, sprawled on the tabletop from exhaustion and exhilaration. Zeke collapsed on my back while his dick flinched against my fleshy walls. We rested in that position for a moment to minimize the impending mess we were about to make.

I grabbed a handful of tissues from the box on the vanity and handed them to him. Unhurriedly, he slid his limpness out of my ocean, cupping his hand around his manhood to catch the stray semen. *We are so damn nasty,* I thought, as I snickered.

"What's funny?" His brow pinched as he concentrated on cleaning me.

"Us. This," I said, still hunched over, glaring at him in the mirror. "Me being a whole hoe again."

"Nah. Never that. Maybe this is the type of shit that happens when you are somebody's girlfriend," he uttered, lightly slapping my ass before wiping me clean.

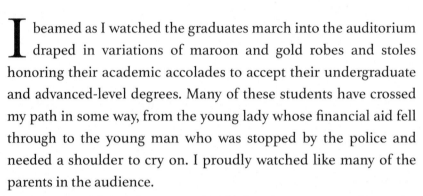

I beamed as I watched the graduates march into the auditorium draped in variations of maroon and gold robes and stoles honoring their academic accolades to accept their undergraduate and advanced-level degrees. Many of these students have crossed my path in some way, from the young lady whose financial aid fell through to the young man who was stopped by the police and needed a shoulder to cry on. I proudly watched like many of the parents in the audience.

My gaze glanced over to Ezekiel, who was seated on the opposite side of the stage. He flashed me a sexy closed-mouth smile, and I discreetly retorted with a twinkle of my own. My damn thong was already purposeless from our rendezvous just a few minutes ago, and here it was, getting soaked again.

Maxine was positioned next to me as we watched the graduates cross the stage. She whispered, "Mmhmm. Where did you disappear to? Your ass smells like sex and sin."

I snickered, balling a fist to my mouth to conceal my grin.

"Oh, what an aroma. Let me bottle this shit up," I whispered through a chuckle.

I caught Ezekiel's glare again, and he teasingly shook his head, chastising me for being chatty. I blushed, feigning innocence as I pursed my lips to prevent my beam.

Maxine nudged me and uttered, "Q."

I peered into the audience where faculty and staff were seated to see Quinton's fiery leer dart between Ezekiel and me. My ex-husband showed his ass during our separation, but he'd been downright unruly since the divorce. His negative energy was not always directed toward me; however, it impacted me because of this situation's impact on our daughter.

Shiloh was infuriated, and her wrath was primarily directed at

Quinton. She recoiled from her father, and Quinton tried to use me as his intermediary... His ally. The circumstance was a lot to process for all of us but for Shi, her world as she knew it was collapsing... And her daddy was the cause.

A nother commencement was in the books for my tenure at Monroe University. I cried and laughed with the students and even joined the circle to serenade the graduates who were members of my sorority.

"Jemma."

I heard Quinton's voice behind me as I hugged a few more graduates. Once the crowd cleared, I turned around to acknowledge him. He looked good. His monochromatic camel-hued ensemble suited his athletic physique very well. I snickered at the attention he received from women as I watched him approach me.

"Quinton. Hey," I said, the smile I previously had diminished at the sight of his despondent expression.

"Hey, Jem. You good?" he asked, and it appeared to pain him.

"I am. How are you?"

"Surviving," he practically growled.

I wanted to roll my eyes, but I stood steadfast with a neutral guise.

"You called me. What's up?" he muttered.

"I called you over a week ago, Quinton."

"And I texted you that I'd call you back when I had a chance. This is the chance," he smugly uttered.

I exhaled and shook my head.

"I was calling because Shiloh's therapist is recommending a few joint sessions with us," I inhaled to quell my irritation.

"Are you sure it was the therapist's recommendation or yours?

This sounds like some shit you would put in Shi's head," he contested accusatorily.

"Quinton, I'm not doing this with you. Yes or no. Will you go to the therapy session for Shiloh?" I probe, desperate to terminate this interaction.

"Of course, Jemma. I'll do anything to get my babygirl back on track. Send me the details," he requested.

An awkward moment of silence lingered between us like a quiet storm. Quinton's green eyes used to be like kryptonite, my weakness, but now they were just shallow capsules that held lies and deceit for so many years.

The bass of powerful footsteps and the familiar fragrance of Creed cologne pleasantly disrupted my daze. If my ex-husband was my kryptonite, then *my boyfriend* was vibranium, indestructible, my very own Black Panther.

"Coach," Ezekiel greeted me with a nod while approaching me and Quinton. "Dr. Holiday, a moment?" Ezekiel asked, focusing his stare on me.

I had to control my breathing before facing him in an attempt to subdue the thump in my kitty. This man's finesse turned me into putty... Every damn time.

"Dr. Green. What can I do for you?" I asked.

I hiked my brows, hoping the action would minimize the twinkle in my eyes.

"Dr. Green, I am not done talking to my -" Quinton's impending announcement faded, and indignation laced his face.

"Jemma and I are still speaking. Oh, wait, my bad, do I need to get your approval now? I need permission to speak to my ex-wife? My daughter's mother?" Quinton indignantly questioned.

Ezekiel scoffed, swiping a hand down his beard.

"Nah, Coach. No permission necessary. Dr. Holiday knows

where to find me when she's done. Correct," Zeke turned to me with lifted eyebrows.

I nodded to confirm my understanding.

His hand brushed my forearm and then a light squeeze as he flashed the sweetest smile, then said, "When you're done, I would love a moment of your time."

I nodded again, uselessly trying to contain a modicum of composure and professional decorum. But Ezekiel caused the most unscrupulous, immoral penetration through my center with the simplest touch.

Quinton was practically invisible to me because I forgot he was standing there as I watched Zeke slowly amble away with so much swag and certainty.

"You're fucking ridiculous, Jemma," Quinton snarled.

He stepped closer to me, sneering through clenched teeth.

"You falling for the first nigga to show you interest... Really? Our history can never be erased, J. I don't give a damn who you *think* you call yourself loving," he *tsk*ed.

A callous expression fancied my face because his same sad song was getting real old. I snickered with a closed-mouth, smug grin.

"You're absolutely right, Quinton. Our history can never be erased. But my future..." My voice trailed off, darting my eyes toward Dr. Green, who was conversing with a group of students. "My future is bright, transformed, and made anew."

I started to walk away but then paused my exit. Closing the short distance between us, I uttered, "And don't get it twisted, he wasn't the first to show interest. I just did what a married person was supposed to do when approached by the opposite sex... Say no thank you. I'll see you in two weeks, Quinton. Have a blessed day."

2

ZEKE

Coach Holiday was begging for an ass-whooping. I barked
mutedly as I walked into the room where I'd just consumed
a taste of my Jules. Every time I encountered that man, I always
had to maintain a level of civility. Honestly, I had more to lose than
he did at this point in the game, namely Jemma, but it didn't
change the fact that I wanted to beat that nigga's ass.

This was my first time seeing him since he approached me at
the coffee shop a couple months ago. But I'd heard enough from
Jules about how he'd been acting like a bitch with her concerning
a few unresolved business items from their divorce.

But on campus, Coach had been sequestered, and for good
reason. The rumors that were circulating around campus about
him fathering a child with another woman had now been
confirmed as reality. Although it seemed that Coach and his baby's
mother, Bethany, were only co-parenting, she was not going away
quietly. To Quinton's dismay, she disclosed details of their
relationship and the paternity of her daughter to anyone who
would listen.

Shortly after the divorce, Quinton occasionally overstepped his bounds by stopping by Jemma's place unannounced. That behavior quickly ended the day I answered her door. I'd been ready for the smoke with that nigga, but we both acquiesced when Jemma stepped between our bloodthirsty leers. I gave the coach a few simple departing words to ensure we were clear on our positions in Jemma's life. *'Tread lightly, Coach. She's mine.'*

The only communication with Jemma now pertained to Shiloh and her well-being. Their daughter was not taking the divorce well at all. And given her current state, Jules didn't want to add any additional abnormalities to her daughter's new normal. Mainly our relationship.

Since spring break, when I confessed my love for Jemma, and she returned the sentiment, we'd been in a covert undercover relationship... And I hated that shit. We alternated weekends at each other's homes or sneaked off to a cabin about an hour from Monroe, but the situationship was getting old. Jemma said that *I* was *her man,* and dammit, that's what I wanted to be. Publicly.

Thankfully, the light taps at the door momentarily interrupted my petulance.

"It's open," I announced while perched on the sofa across the room.

Sleek, bouncy, auburn-hued tendrils attached to the prettiest face appeared in the doorway.

"Hey," she whispered with a coy expression on her face.

"Hey," I returned.

"Can I come in?" she asked, peering right to left down the hallway, seemingly checking for any oglers.

"Of course."

She entered, closed the door, and leaned against it, gaping at me with narrowed eyes. I stared right back at her cute ass. Earlier, I was so desperate to be inside of her that I didn't notice how the yellow dress hugged her curvy frame. I bit my bottom lip and crooked my finger, beckoning her to me. Jemma locked the door and practically floated across the room.

No surprise to me, Jules climbed on my lap to straddle me. She could always sense when I was tense, as I could decipher when she was in her head, so this stance offered dual satisfaction. Not sexual, but intimate, passionate... Shit, kindredly connected. Jemma understood my need for closeness, and I comprehended her desire for assurance, especially if her wack-ass ex filled her head with uncertainty.

With our foreheads coupled, we simultaneously exhaled deeply and then softly kissed. Words of affirmation were not necessary for us; we committed to demonstrating action.

"Have dinner with me tonight." I felt her breath hitch against my chest. "At my place, of course." I continued, not in the mood to fight about being in public.

"I don't know. I need to check on Shi," she whispered through an exasperated breath.

"Go check on Shiloh first, then -"

Jemma put a finger to my lips to cease my words and recited, "Don't think, don't hesitate, just come." She smiled, parroting my typical guidance.

I smiled, then nodded.

"Yeah, baby. Just come and I'll take care of the rest."

After another fifteen minutes of kissing and fondling each other, we finally exited the room to face the reality of post-graduation events. I had to make an appearance at a few receptions before both Jemma, and I spoke at the alumni event. We strolled down the hall, focused on our phones, when we heard a voice that caused us both to groan in frustration.

"Dr. Green, I've been searching all over for you," Christina Hall, the university's Chief of Staff, stated. "You have fifteen minutes before your next commitment," she sang, tapping her watch to emphasize the obvious.

Christina repeatedly darted curious eyes between Jemma and me.

"Dr. Holiday. Hello. We always seem to need Dr. Green at the same time. What a coinky-dink," she jeered, lifting her eyebrows, then swiped the long hair from her shoulder.

"A coincidence indeed, Ms. Hall," Jemma said with a bit of sarcasm in her tone. "He's all yours."

"Well, wouldn't that make me a lucky girl?" Ms. Hall chuckled, placing a hand on my shoulder after tossing that faux-looking hair again.

Jules sniggered dismissively, and it took everything in me not to laugh.

"I will see you both at the alumni reception." Jemma nodded, then sashayed down the hall.

I tried my best not to look at her ass, but I was confident that I did a piss poor job at containing my gaze.

"Dr. Green," Ms. Hall announced, trying to gain my attention.

Once Jules disappeared from my view, I shifted my head to Ms. Hall with a manufactured smile.

"Shall we?" she confirmed.

"Um, yes, we shall."

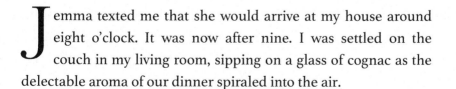

Jemma texted me that she would arrive at my house around eight o'clock. It was now after nine. I was settled on the couch in my living room, sipping on a glass of cognac as the delectable aroma of our dinner spiraled into the air.

I'd hired a chef to prepare the seafood pasta and lobster bisque that was warming in my oven. I had to figure out how to repress my chagrin before she arrived because I was confident her tardiness was due to something pertaining to Shiloh. Her daughter had been downright depressed and defiant lately, and she was taking it out on her father *and* mother.

I heard the rumble of the garage door open and immediately closed my eyes to control my breathing. Lagging-heeled footsteps clanked, then silent tip-toeing ensured. Jemma had the same routine when she entered my house; remove her shoes, hang her bag on the hook in the hallway, then amble to find me. When I felt her enter the great room, I stood from the couch and turned to greet her. Immediately, my disdain disappeared in response to her reddened eyes and flushed cheeks.

"Jules. What's wrong?" I asked, strolling to meet her in the center of the living room.

Her honey-hued, wide eyes were so discouraged. Reaching to clutch her nape, I stroked my thumb up and down her skin to help her mellow.

"I'm just so worried about her," Jemma uttered, voice trembling.

"Baby, come and sit."

I rested my hand on the small of her back, escorting her to the couch. No directive was required because Jules automatically positioned herself on my lap.

"What happened?" I probed further, continuing to gently massage her neck and shoulders.

"Nothing different. It just breaks my heart to see her light dimmed like this. Shiloh is so angry. Not eating. Barely speaking to me. That definitely hurts me the most," she said as I thumbed away a stray tear. "Shi and I tell each other everything. She's my daughter and my friend. But right now I just feel like her worst enemy. Maybe second to her father."

Jemma blew out an exasperated breath and leaned her head on my shoulder.

"I'm so sorry, Jemma. I'm glad she agreed to the counseling though. Maybe she can express some things to you both with the therapist's support. This is a lot of change for her."

She nodded.

We settled in necessary silence for several long heartbeats. Her erratic breaths against my neck started to calm. Jules remained snuggled into my neck, and I would hold on to her for as long as she needed me.

"Thank you," she mumbled against my nape.

"No need to thank me, baby," I cupped two fingers under her chin to kiss those pouty lips. "You hungry?" I asked.

She shook her head.

"The rumble in your belly is telling me something different," I teased, kissing against her cheek.

"Something does smell delicious," she said, shifting her body to sit up.

"Come on. Let's get you fed, OK?"

"Ok," she whined like my spoiled Jules.

In mere months I'd ruined this woman for any other man who attempted to follow behind me. I chuckled, patting her behind to lift her from my lap. I stood, towering over Jemma, but that didn't prevent me from grasping my hands around and cuddling into her neck. I guided her into the kitchen, refusing to unshackle from our coupling.

I watched a faint smile curve Jemma's lips as she admired the fancy setup in the dining room. Blood-orange and red roses were centered on the table. A bottle of her favorite red wine from

Toussaint Winery, tossed salad to accompany the seafood feast, and a small black box with a red bow was positioned in front of her place setting.

"Uh oh, is this box going to be like the last time?" Jemma questioned through a snicker.

I laughed, thinking about the *last time*. When Jules came to New York for the new year, I gifted her with a box filled with goodies to heighten our sexual experience. If I wasn't already in love with Jemma Jule Holiday, my ass definitely fell head over heels after that night of salacious intimacy.

"Nah, not this time. But I'm not opposed to playing with some toys later." I winked. "Let's eat first. You can open this gift after dinner."

"Zee," she whined again.

I chuckled and instructed, "Eat, beautiful."

We listlessly talked about nothing and everything. Jemma and I became more acquainted and familiar with each other every day by simply observing one another. Like how she preferred her protein on a separate plate from her side dishes. Or how she knew that I preferred my cognac with a twist of lemon. Our relationship was becoming routine but not in an ordinary way. Every night created new love stories, and every morning unique memoirs were etched in my psyche.

"How's Mrs. Green?" Jemma asked, indulging in a sip of wine.

"Mom is better. Hard-headed but better," I chortled.

My mother battled the coronavirus for several weeks and couldn't escape the vigorous cough. One day when my cousin Myron was visiting, mom was having chest pains, and he immediately called an ambulance. Her oxygen levels were low, but thankfully, the pains were due to the chronic cough. It wasn't ideal, but I flew to New York the week before graduation to place my eyes on her instead of getting second-hand information.

"She was really about to fix Sunday dinner two days after being released from the hospital," I muttered, shaking my head. "Ezra's crazy ass actually put a stool in front of the sink for her to sit on so that she could clean the greens."

"Oh my goodness. That sounds like Ezra," she chuckled.

Jemma and my brother Ezra's relationship started off a little rocky due to his overprotection of me during Jemma's unresolved marital situation. Now that he sees I'm happier than I'd been in a very long time, Ezra and Jules were establishing cordiality.

"You know our mothers think they are superwomen. I'm glad you went to see her. You wouldn't have been able to rest," she tossed me a quick wink.

I procrastinated when deciding whether to go to New York, but Jemma sternly convinced me to leave. *You'll never forgive yourself if, God forbid, anything more serious happened to her.* And she was right. When my father got sick four years ago, I returned from a work trip just hours after he died. To this day, I still question my decision to take that last meeting. Maybe if I would've left, I could have said goodbye.

Jemma cleared the plates from the table as I retrieved the dessert from the refrigerator. Pouring her another glass of wine, I transported the dessert tray and our beverages to the cocktail table, along with her gift box.

"Ok, so what's in the box, Dr. Green?" she demanded.

"So impatient, Dr. Holiday. Let's make a toast first."

"Ezekiel!" She giggled, but the eye roll was a clear indication of annoyance.

"No seriously, Jules. I want to make a toast then I promise you can open your gift."

She shook her head but then nodded, lifting her glass.

"Here's to my first year as Provost of Monroe University. I can't believe the school year has come to a close. Never would I have imagined this whirlwind experience. If you recall the first day that we met, I said that you were *an experience*, Jemma. And this is exactly what I was meaning. You have been a friend, a mentor, a colleague, a partner, and an unimaginable love. Here's to many more *experiences* together, beautiful. Cheers."

"Cheers," she whispered, blinking away the dewiness in her eyes.

We connected our glasses and then shared a kiss. Jemma peered at me with a visage of longing and love. After a few sips of wine, she leaned into me, allowing her lips to caper against mine. The wine and cognac mingled delectably as she scattered a few soft kisses before lending me her tongue. My manhood was ready to get the party started.

"Zeke," Jemma said questioningly before sucking my tongue into her mouth.

"Hmm," I groaned, barely coherent.

"Can I open my gift now?" She giggled, releasing my tongue, and then kissed the tip of my nose.

I shook my head and motioned to the box. Jules giddily obliged, doing a little shimmy as she reached across the table. I laughed at the goofy grin on her face as she slowly tugged the velvet ribbon as if it was delicate. Lifting the box, she dramatically shook it before removing the top.

Jemma's brow furrowed once she peeled back the red tissue paper revealing a small black velvet bag. She looked at me, and I lifted my brow, encouraging her to keep going. Jemma opened the bag and retrieved a key attached to a silver keychain in the shape of the sun and moon.

"Zeke, a key," she stated curiously.

Jemma's face was imprinted with confusion because she already had a key to my house.

"Yes, a key," I provided no additional details to her displeasure. Jemma rolled her eyes.

"A key to what, babe?"

"Jules, I told you that I would find a place that's still and quiet, just for us. A place where we can just be mindless and free. *This* is the key to that place," I pointed at the silver metal she twirled between her fingers.

"What? Where? New York?" She probed, beaming with excitement and anticipation.

"Florida."

"Florida," she repeated questioningly. "Keys to your place... in Key West?" she asked, the inquisitive stare continued.

I leered at Jemma like she was crazy. She knew that my ex-wife and I maintained our vacation home in Key West, Florida, as a place to take vacations with our kids... Separately, of course. When neither of us occupied the home, we leased it and banked the profits for EJ and Eriya. So I was a little disturbed by Jemma's thought process. What type of nigga would I be to take her to where I and my ex once resided?

"No, Jules. I'm not even sure why you would think that," I scoffed.

"This is the key to *our* place, baby, on Anna Maria Island. It's a condo on the Ritz Carlton privately owned property directly on the beach. Just for me and you." I swiped the tip of her nose and flashed a slight smile.

I'd been eyeing the property for months after Jemma, and I spent the best seven days of my life together in New York earlier this year. Jemma and I had become the master of getaways in the Monroe area since that was the only way we could truly be together outside of our homes. Her family had a cabin in Brighton Falls not too far from Monroe that we'd visited frequently, and we found a quaint, secluded bed and breakfast right outside of town. But I wanted a serene getaway retreat that we could call our own. This was a big move seeing as Jemma was only my girlfriend. An incognito girlfriend at that, so I was nervous as hell about her reaction.

"Zeke, you bought this place?" Her pretty honey eyes bulged, flipping through the papers I handed her.

I nodded.

"For-for us, babe," she stuttered, covering her mouth with one hand, vainly attempting to repress the tear.

Jemma continued to nervously twiddle the key over and over between her fingertips. I placed my hand over hers, halting her jitters. Cupping her chin, I faintly smiled, swiping away the tear that salted the corner of her mouth.

"I need time with you, Jules. I know that is complicated for you here in Monroe, but I can't keep sneaking around."

"We are not sneaking, Zeke," she said sadly, interrupting me.

"We are most *definitely* sneaking if I can't take my woman to dinner within the city limits. If I can't kiss you when I want or hug you when my heart desires. Shit, grab your ass if that's what I'm feeling," I chuckled, but my tone was serious. "I have to gaze at you from a distance, Jemma, wishing I can be close to you. That shit doesn't work for me anymore."

"Zee, baby, I'm sorry. I-"

"Shh," I hushed her ensuing explanation.

"No need to apologize, sweetheart. I willingly signed on the dotted line to be entangled with your complication. But I need you, Jemma, outside of these four walls," I uttered, and the urgency in my tenor could not be ignored. "What do you say, baby?"

Jemma gently stroked her fingertips down the center of my

face, then leaned in to give me the softest, most sensual, and most loving kiss.

"I say yes," she whispered, resting her forehead against mine. "I love you, Zee."

"Jules, I love you more than you'll ever know."

3

JULES

"Girl, he did what?" Maxine and Quaron sang loudly in unison.

"He bought a vacation condo so that we can be together... alone. No roaming eyes, chatter, or distractions," I said, still in disbelief.

"Why do you sound like you're still trying to *decide* if you're going?" Maxi queried, eyes bulging in shock.

"Um, heffa, what time is the flight? I'm on my way to help your ass pack," Quaron declared, mirroring Maxine's bewildered expression.

I was perched in the lounge chair on the balcony of Ezekiel's bedroom, talking to my two crazy friends on FaceTime. The sun was just beginning to rise, and I texted them because I could not sleep. For whatever reason, they were awake at the ungodly hour as well. I knew exactly why I was unable to sleep... Ezekiel's gift.

I awakened before the moon drifted to make space for the sun. And what did I do?... Stargaze at him. He was a beautiful man. Skin, the hue of hot cocoa, swaddled an exquisitely muscled body.

Hooded brown eyes led to a distinguished nose. I smiled at the slight pout of his pillowy soft lips that wantonly scrutinized every curve of my body last night. Closing my eyes, I meditated on the sweet melodic buzz of his light snore until my phone's chime disrupted my fantasy. *Maxine and Quaron.*

"I'm going. But a condo... in Florida. That seems like a big commitment."

"Newsflash Jem, you *are* in a committed relationship, honey. Whether at his house or yours, y'all are together almost every damn day. Bitch, you're practically somebody's wife again," Quaron declared.

"Don't you ever let those words leave your mouth again," I threatened. "I'm definitely not ready for that. May *never* be ready for that."

"And does the good doctor know this?" Maxi probed with a scowl on her face.

I stared at their faces in the frames on my phone. Honestly, I wasn't certain if Zeke knew my position on marriage. It was never a topic of discussion. We were just focused on enjoying one another.

"H e knows," I whispered, almost inaudible.

"If you say so," Roni rolled her eyes, unconvinced. "When are you leaving?"

"Two days. We're driving to St. Louis Sunday morning for a late afternoon flight. I want to stay in Monroe to make sure Shiloh has everything she needs for her camping trip."

Maxine nodded.

"You betta, sis. I'm proud of you, Jem," Quaron uttered with a waffling smile.

"Why?" I inquired, brow creased.

"Because you are simply putting one foot in front of the other. Walking through maybe the second toughest season of your life like a boss," Roni uttered, then winked.

We stared at each other for a long minute, quietly reminiscing on the good, bad, and ugly of the past twenty years. Quaron rapidly blinked, seemingly suppressing the looming tears before she lifted her middle finger. I smirked, then crossed my eyes and licked my tongue out at her. Both of us vainly tried to minimize the emotions bubbling in our bellies.

While she wouldn't admit it, Roni was struggling with the divorce. She loved her brother, but she loved me like a blood sister too. Wrong was wrong, and Quaron knew that her brother was dead ass wrong. Quinton tried to be pissed at his sister when she told him the truth about himself, but they were slowly making amends.

Turning to address the rumble in my background, I pressed my lips into thin slits, blushing at the naked Adonis climbing out of bed. *Good Lord.* Zeke rubbed a hand down his bald head, looking around the room before he noticed me on the balcony. He nodded his head, acknowledging me. I blushed, admiring his morning wood as it bobbed up and down, waving hello too. He turned to walk towards the bathroom, and all I could do was shake my head at the way my kitty was doused at the sight of him. *Damn, he's fine!*

"Um, heffa, we know he's fine. We've seen that man," Maxi rolled her eyes.

"Did I say that aloud?" I asked, more to myself than them.

"He must be walking around slanging all of that dick," Roni squealed through a chuckle.

"Roni," I bellowed, eyeballs protruding in response to her vulgarness.

"Chile, if that thang is anything like his brother's, I understand why your ass is out here like New Edition, *lost in love*," Quaron said matter-of-factly. "Does it run in the family, Maxi?" she asked, interrogating Maxine about Myron's member.

"I plead the fifth, nasty," Maxine chortled, rolling her eyes.

Glancing behind me again, Zeke stood in the middle of the room, gawking at me. I, on the other hand, was gaping at that dick. My glowing golden skin flushed with embarrassment at the visual of *him* and that glorious penis. A quiver pressed through my body as my eyes darted back to the screen. Roni and Maxi were looking at me as if I was about to let them have a peek.

"Um, you're awful and I gotta go. I'll call y'all before I leave. Love you. Bye." I swiftly ended the call with thing number one and two.

"Jules," Ezekiel's bass-filled tenor rumbled.

I turned to see him leaning against the footboard, massaging his dick.

"I need you," he ordered.

I brightened. Shit, my whole damn body was aflame.

"Coming," I caroled.

Anna Maria Island was absolutely gorgeous. Although my stomach was queasy from the turbulent flight, I was able to admire its allure. The clear, luminous waters stretched for miles as the driver transported us to the hotel. Ezekiel massaged his finger through my hair as I rested on his shoulder.

"Any better?" he whispered.

I nodded.

"The peppermint is helping," I peered up at him with a faux smile.

"We're almost there," he encouraged, rubbing my neck and kissing my forehead.

I lifted, awestricken, as the black Escalade pulled into the circular entryway of the Ritz Carlton Hotel and Private Residences. It did not resemble a traditional Ritz hotel at all. The buildings mimicked luxury apartments surrounded by brilliant blue skies, shimmering sands, and crystalized water. The truck door opened, and we were greeted by a handsome young man holding a silver tray with small bottles of water, a glass of champagne, and a can of ginger ale.

"Dr. Green. Dr. Holiday. Welcome to your home away from home here at the Ritz Carlton," the handsome young man greeted as another gentleman helped me out of the truck.

"Dr. Holiday, I understand that you have an uneasy stomach. The ginger soda will help," he continued, pouring the bubbly liquid over the ice.

I nodded my thanks.

"My name is David and I will be your concierge during your stay. Monroe will take care of your luggage. Please follow me."

Holding hands was not normal for Zeke and me in public, but instinctively, we searched for each other's touch as we strolled into the lobby. I perched on the white couch while Ezekiel signed the paperwork. Since this was our first time on the property, he had to finalize some business before we could enter our new space. David appeared out of nowhere, offering me a small charcuterie board and more ginger ale.

"Thank you, David. Can I ask you a question?"

"Yes ma'am," he answered, intently listening.

"I want to make a special dinner for Dr. Green. A surprise. Can you help with that?" I whispered, eyeing Ezekiel, who was still fully engaged in signing documents.

"Absolutely, Dr. Holiday. Just tell me what you need and when?"

After giving David very specific instructions, I nibbled on the exotic cheeses and nuts while taking in my surroundings. The lobby was decorated in white and gold with hints of bold colors. A wall of sliding doors opened to a massive pool and outdoor bar. The pool appeared to endlessly flow into the ocean. I would definitely need a nap first, but I couldn't wait to take a dip in the ocean.

"Shall we?" Ezekiel asked, extending his hand to help me up.

"We shall."

"I told David we would do the tour later after you've rested. I have some breakfast being brought to the room. Our groceries should be delivered this afternoon. If I missed anything, we can always place another order-"

"Zee, baby, it's fine," I interrupted, gently resting my hand against his abdomen. "Thank you... For everything."

He nodded and kissed my temple. I loved that Zeke was so attentive and always confirmed my preferences, but I wanted him to relax too. To allow me to show him a little attention.

We navigated our way to the private residential building across the corridor from the hotel's regular resort. Zeke swiped the key fob to enter the gated grounds. I gasped at the sizeable antique fountain in the center of the courtyard. It was surrounded by plush greenery, bistro tables, and a full bar. Both the staff and owners sporadically ambled around as breakfast was being served. I examined the gorgeous architecture while deeply inhaling fresh, crisp air. Hand in hand, Zeke and I followed David through an archway when a cool, invigorating breeze brushed across my face. I admired the beach as we drove from the airport, but to see it just a few feet away was breathtaking.

"Here we are," David heralded, signaling for Ezekiel to open the one-eighteen door.

He used the same key fob to unlock the door, and we stepped into a sunken foyer before walking up a few steps. My breath was immediately snatched away again.

A wall of glass sliding doors opened to an outdoor living area and a private pool. *Is that a bed?* The pool had a damn bed floating in the center. I made a mental note to investigate further after we completed our tour of the property. A high-end, modern walnut and white-colored kitchen was to the left, and a six-seat dining room table was to the right. A white leather sectional faced a large wall-mounted television hanging over an electric fireplace. The short hallway led us to two beautifully decorated small bedrooms with a jack-and-jill bathroom in the middle. I wondered if these were the only living quarters, but I didn't ask any questions.

David directed us up a short flight of steps while he stood at the bottom. Ezekiel slid the barn-style bamboo door to reveal the most exquisite view I'd ever witnessed. The bedroom decor, the oversized balcony with a hot tub and shower, the beachfront view... It was resplendent.

"So what do you think?" Ezekiel asked, smizing with his eyes because I believe he already knew the answer.

I spun to connect with his delightful irises because I needed him to know I meant every word I was about to say.

"I think it's incredible. Zee, *you're* incredible," I affirmed breathily, closing the short distance between us.

Wrapping my arms around his waist, I tossed my head back and whispered, "You've been *everything* I didn't know I needed."

.   .   .

W e conked out after receiving our luggage and enjoyed a light breakfast. I jolted from my sleep when the phone rang. Groggily, I answered because Zeke didn't stir. David was calling to ask if he could bring our groceries to the condo. The man of the house gave me specific instructions to wake him up when the food was being delivered.

"David seems cool and all, but I want to be up when the delivery guy gets here," he said right before burying his head under a pillow.

Following directions, I delicately nibbled his ear, causing him to groan.

"Babe. The groceries are ready."

He nodded his head while still nestled below the pillow.

"Use your words, Dr. Green." I teased.

"I'm getting up," he stated but didn't move.

Then the doorbell sounded.

"I'm up," he grunted this time and sat up in bed.

I giggled at the crumpled folds in his face as he shifted his lengthened erection. I guess he called himself trying to tame the beast before walking down the steps, but that girthy mammoth was never compliant.

Following behind him, I tightened my robe before descending the stairs. Zeke opened the door, and David appeared with a smile. He instructed the delivery person and confirmed our plans for dinner by the pool. Residence owners had the luxury of using the neighboring resort amenities while enjoying the solitude of their private domicile.

After putting the groceries away, I grabbed the drink Zeke had prepared for me and joined him on the patio. He was inclined on the floating mattress, bathing in the sun. Gazing up at me, he smiled, immediately opening his legs for me to settle between them. I leaned back, resting in the comfort of his arms. Soft jazz played through the surround sound speakers.

It was a little after four o'clock, and the sun was still blazing, but we were in chill mode. The patio had motorized screens to block the sun, but we opted to soak in the rays. Operation decompress was in full effect. We didn't speak or stir. We simply allowed the mellow rhythmic beats of our hearts to do the talking. Zeke and I needed this... Respite, tranquility, refuge.

"I may never leave this place," I chuckled as he lazily stroked his knuckles against my cheek. "The resort is beautiful and I want to see what the island has to offer, but this. Us like this..." I sighed in a relaxed manner as my words momentarily faded. "I don't want it to end," I whispered almost inaudibly.

"It doesn't have to end, Jules. This is our place. Anytime we need to reset individually or together, we can do it here. But right now we have seven days of bliss to enjoy each other wherever and however we choose." Zeke bit my neck and then kissed away the sting.

"Wherever we choose? Even right here?" I probed teasingly.

He nodded.

"Even right here, baby," Zeke said in a raspy tone.

"Hmm, let me see if you're keeping it one hundred with me," I bantered.

I placed my glass on the side table and repositioned my body to face him before drizzling soft kisses from his bald head down his bare chest. I loosened the belt on my robe, exposing my naked frame. My breasts glistened from the shea butter I applied after my shower. They were heavy with need, among other things.

The lustful grin at the corner of his mouth was evidence of his gratification. He massaged my hardened nipples before idling his head between my mounds. I kissed and licked his nape as he laggardly circled my areolas with his tongue. This man sucked my titties like he was breastfeeding. But I was the hungry one, famished for his weightiness to appease my appetite.

Fingering the band of his shorts, I tapped his thigh, instructing him to lift so I could uncage the animal that had been clawing up my back earlier. Zeke loved when I tickled his navel with my tongue because he knew what was next. Preparing for the forthcoming salacious behavior, he retrieved the remote from the side table. He lowered the shades, which made the patio completely private.

I perched between his muscular legs that were lazily draped across the bed. With my legs crisscrossed, I leaned down, kissing the tip of his glistening member. As the sun initiated its descent in the background, so did my mouth, sliding down the slope of his smooth veiny dick. I happily moaned, gladdened by the immeasurable intrusion against my tongue.

Since our first sexual encounter months ago, the night my world turned upside down, Ezekiel taught me the art of building the orgasm one stroke, maneuver, and lick at a time. In his words, *don't think, don't hesitate, just come.* And *cum* was exactly what I wanted him to do.

I filled my cheeks with every inch of him until I was almost breathless. Slowly bobbing my head up and down, I repeated the perfected motion to ensure the carnal result I sought. A fluent glide on the downstroke, followed by an unyielding suction on the upstroke, always did the trick.

"Ju - Ju - Jules. Damn, woman," Ezekiel groaned, inspecting my every move. "Look at me, baby."

Got him! I silently declared victory because the explosion would be epic once we connected eye to eye with his dick dallying in my mouth.

"Mmm," I moaned, irises wide and focused.

I tightly pursed my lips around his width, refusing to cease the salacious flow.

"Jemma. Fuck," he yelped, grunting his words through gritted teeth.

Climax. Ezekiel reached a ferocious conclusion with fists full of my braids clutched in his hands. Shit, I practically reached the pinnacle from his wanton enthusiasm alone. I gazed at him, savoring every minute of his afterglow as I lightly caressed his diminishing erection until he calmed. He swiped a finger across my lips, ridding my mouth of any leftover remnants of *him*.

"Come here," he uttered gruffly.

I immediately obliged, climbing the length of his stately frame. Vigorously grasping the back of my head, Zeke ogled me before kissing my lips with so much passion and purpose I wanted to weep. He lowered his hand beside us and pulled the lever to fully recline the bed.

"Let me kiss those other lips," he proposed, directing me up his body.

In the past several months, I'd become accustomed to climbing this man like a damn tree. He reveled in being smothered by my voluptuous thighs. When my kitty reached the tip of his lips, Ezekiel closed his eyes and whispered, "Amen."

I lowered my head, glaring at him with a questioning furrow.

"Just expressing my gratitude for this delicious meal," he answered my unspoken query.

Amen! My head fell back as my eyes lazily closed. I immediately shut the hell up to allow this man to feast because I did not want him to miss a drop. He tongue-kissed my pussy to a listless, undemanding pace. But it was his low, husky growl of satisfaction that completely leveled me.

"Mmm," he moaned.

"Oh my fucking goodness. Dr. Green," I bayed, just as the light from the sun separated to form a magnificent rainbow.

4

ZEKE

It was our fifth day in paradise, and yes, I was reluctantly counting down the days until we had to leave. If I had any doubts about securing this place for Jemma and me, they had quickly faded to nothing. I'd been so damn nervous about the investment for the two of us, but so far, it was money well spent.

The past week I'd been able to explore my Jules in a manner that only resided in my dreams. She was so carefree, unbothered, and downright bubbly. A simple glance or kiss on her cheek triggered boisterous jovial laughter. Jules radiated daily, and I loved this for her. Shit, I loved this for *us*.

The chatter on the golf course shortened my daydream. I took my put and chuckled, recalling Jemma giving me *permission* to golf this morning. She literally said *you have my permission to go,* after I sucked her clit until it was swollen, and she was dazed.

I booked her a deluxe spa package to enjoy while I was gone. While we'd thoroughly enjoyed each other's company during the day and coupled our bodies nightly, we understood the importance of *me time*.

Yesterday, we finally ventured off the property and rented a convertible to drive up the coast of Anna Maria Island. I'd arranged lunch under the waterfall and horseback riding on the beach as the sunset. Jules was so damn beautiful as the moon illuminated her pretty face when she slept during our drive back to the condo.

"Dr. Green, join us for another nine holes," Dr. Lomax extended an invitation.

Jemma and I met Dr. Timothy Lomax and his wife, Vanessa, at the pool a couple nights ago. They were a slightly older couple who'd been long-time owners at the resort.

"I would love to, Dr. Lomax, but I have a beautiful woman waiting for me. I promised her I would be back for an early dinner."

"Understood. Well if you two get a chance, join us for brunch tomorrow. It's mine and my wife's thirty-five year anniversary," he exclaimed.

"Congratulations. Happy Anniversary. What's your secret?" I questioned, tossing my golf bag on my shoulder.

"To show up for each other every time. Shit, and say *I love you* even when times are rough," he answered without hesitation.

"That simple?" I confirmed.

"That simple," Dr. Lomax retorted with certainty etched across his face.

I rode back to the resort and parted ways from the other golfers in the lobby. Jemma was probably napping after the salt scrubs, jet bath, massage, and a host of other services I ordered for her.

Approaching our condo, I heard the smooth melodies of R&B music. Quietly, I opened the door and climbed the two steps into the great room, and there she was. Jemma was wearing a copper-colored silk spaghetti-strap dress almost the same color as her sunbathed skin. The fabric kissed her flesh perfectly, and it was just thin enough for me to see the swell of her nipples. Her bare ass jiggled as she swayed to the music holding a glass of red wine.

I was so focused on the goddamn wonder before me that I didn't immediately notice the fancy setup in the kitchen. She swung around once she detected me staring. The leisurely grin expanding her cheeks was absolutely gorgeous.

Jules extended her arms to me as SWV sang about being weak in the knees. She clutched my hand, encouraging me to spin her around as she continued to croon. And she actually sounded good as hell. Jemma spun out and then twirled her body into my embrace. We locked eyes, and she cupped the curves of my face while her raspy alto sang from her gut.

♫ *"Your love is so sweet, it knocks me right off of my feet.*
Can't explain why your love, it makes me weak." ♫

"Hey, handsome," she cooed, planting a soft kiss on my lips.

"Hello, gorgeous," I patted her ass to the rhythm of the beat. "What is all of this?" I asked, nestling into her neck, scented with the Gucci Bloom perfume I gave her.

"A dinner date," Jemma beamed.

"Oh, really," I turned her around to press her ass into my already expanded erection.

"Mmhmm. We're going to cook dinner together, take a swim, and then I have a little surprise," she uttered.

Jemma kissed me, then gently pushed my arm, encouraging me to get upstairs to shower. The slap to my ass caused me to turn around and ogle her.

"I keep telling you, Dr. Holiday. I will *fuck* you," I asserted, and I meant that shit.

"Please and thank you, Dr. Green," she teased.

I could have definitely won the award for the fastest shower in history. I cleaned the pertinent areas and hopped out of the shower, and tossed on some shorts and a tank top. Standing at the top of the steps, I shook my head, admiring this alluring woman once again.

Walking into the kitchen, I was welcomed with a glass of cognac and a kiss. My Jules encompassed all five love languages, but she reveled in physical touch, and so did I. Every opportunity we had, we kissed, caressed, and fondled, non-verbally communicating our adoration for each other. Intimacy took precedence over everything, including sex. I constantly craved being buried inside her dripping essence, but the passion and foreplay made the lovemaking spectacular.

A smorgasbord of ingredients was measured and spread across the kitchen island in small bowls. Two balls of dough were rolled out on cast iron skillets, and a large salad bowl was filled with greenery. Jemma was nibbling on cheese while slicing toppings for the salad.

"Can you guess what we're making?" she queried, eyes bright with excitement.

"Hmm," I said, tapping my pointer finger against my chin. "Pizza?" I guessed.

"Not just pizza, my love," she muttered, beating her fingers against the counter like a drum before unveiling the only covered ingredient on display. "Black truffle pizza," Jemma squealed.

"Are you serious?" I damn near squealed right back.

She giddily nodded.

"You want me to fuck you real good don't you," I groaned into her ear.

We cooked, petted, and played with each other like spirited teenagers. Whether it was a slight touch on the arm or a faint graze on the ass, our bodies were instinctively captivated. Connected. The energy between us sometimes baffled me because we melded to each other like familiar old friends.

Jemma had the outdoor dining table decorated with candles and fresh flowers. We ate dinner just as the sun was setting, permitting the moon and stars to have a chance to glow.

What I loved about this condo was the privacy. Although we had a fantastic ocean view from the lanai, passersby could not see into our space. Jemma cleared the table and took the plates into the kitchen. I wasn't ready for the apple fritter dessert we made, so Jemma brought me another drink and a cigar instead.

When she strolled through the sliding doors, my damn mouth dropped to the floor because I was drooling. My Jules was butt-ass naked with my cigar dangling from her lips. She stroked the torch, igniting the flame to light the cigar. Jemma puffed a few times, and it was the sexiest shit I'd ever witnessed. The way her lips wrapped around the Cuban stick and the haze whirling in front of her beautiful face, I was in a fucking trance.

Jemma crossed the short distance to stand before me, and I could not resist running my hand up her bare thigh. I sat up in my chair to kiss, then licked her navel before she passed me the cigar.

Reaching to draw her closer to me, I conceded, "I think I'm ready for my dessert after all."

She playfully withdrew, dodging my attempts to taste her kitty. Jules stepped her bodacious unclad body into the pool and crooked her finger to invite me to join. She didn't have to tell me twice. I removed my clothes and hastily hopped my ass into the pool.

The pool was no more than five feet deep, so I towered over Jemma with only half of my body submerged. She played coy, eluding my attempts to grab her ass and wrap my mouth around her breasts when I dipped my whole frame under the water.

"Jules, baby, are you telling me no?" I checked. Correction, a nigga was whining. "You see what you do to me?" I guided her hand to feel my swollen manhood.

"Let me take care of that for you," she murmured.

Jemma sluggishly tongue-kissed me while swiveling her hand in circular movements around my dick. She whispered in my ear, "Get on the bed."

I was enjoying my position but eager to see what was next. Following directions, I climbed onto the floating mattress in the pool, allowing enough room for her to crawl on. My dick was standing at attention like a flagpole. Jules tip-toed to me and kissed the tip of my dick. She gazed those big almond eyes up at me while languidly guzzling each and every inch of my girth.

Damn!

Jemma hopped onto the bed, settling between my legs. Sweeping her braids to the side, I trailed my tongue down the length of her spine. I swaddled my arms around her to firmly pinch her breast. Jules heaved. Her pants were slow yet frantic.

"Rise up a little, baby," I instructed.

Heeding my request, Jules pressed both hands into my thighs for leverage and thrust her body upward. On her descent, I guided my dick into her slippery folds. Her ass unhurriedly pounded against my thighs... *reverse cowgirl*. The leisurely pace reached a feverish velocity as my strength grew stronger and longer inside her.

"Jules," I moaned, tossing my head back like a bitch.

"Mmhmm," she hummed.

I gripped her hair and practically wrapped a collection of braids around my hand. This woman was lapping my shit from the tip to my balls on repeat.

"Jemma. Jules. Baby. I can't. Fuck. Baby. Shit," I heaved, almost ready to pass the hell out from the lascivious titillation.

Gripping her hips, I roughly pulled her onto her knees, never severing the wanton bond. We were in a dirty duel, and my Jules was winning. She challenged me thrash for thrash, pound for pound. Jemma was unrelenting and my fucking undoing.

Closing my eyes, I surrendered, coming so damn hard that my grunt bellowed as if I was in pain. Labored breathing, I opened my eyes, and all I saw were white spots. Maybe I'd died and gone to heaven. I collapsed backward on the bed, bringing Jemma with me. I encased my naked frame around her and rested peacefully in the bliss of Jemma mutherfucking Holiday.

5

ZEKE & JULES

Zeke

"Lil, what's up, bro? It's been a minute." My brother's baritone boomed in my ear pod.

I'd just finished a workout in the hotel gym while Jemma was gone to lunch with friends. We'd been back from Florida for two days and were staying at the Four Seasons Hotel in downtown St. Louis. Neither of us had to be back in Monroe for another week, so we decided to extend our time together in her hometown. Monroe City was beautiful, but it was a bit boring without the bustle of students filling the streets.

"Big, what's up man? I told you I would be off the grid for a bit. Is Ma ok?" I asked, nervous that my mother may have taken ill again.

"Yeah, yeah, she's good. Getting her strength back slowly but surely. How was Florida?" Ezra questioned.

"Shit, in a word... fucking remarkable," I boasted, chuckling.

"That was two words, but whatever. I asked how Florida was, not Dr. Holiday," Ezra quipped.

"They were both remarkable," I laughed.

The line went quiet for a long minute.

"Hello. Ez," I muttered, trying to determine if we had lost connection.

"Yeah, man. I'm here. Give me a second. I'm just looking up the definition of whipped. Or correction, pussy whipped," he cackled.

"Man, fuck you. Call me what you want as long as it includes Jules."

"Are you back in Monroe?" Ezra continued to probe.

"Nah. St. Louis. I'm staying here until I have to go back to Monroe for the end of year meetings next week."

"Ah, ok. Where is the beautiful Dr. Jemma?" Ezra interrogated me.

"Lunch with some of her line sisters."

"You're in her hood, are you meeting the parents, hanging with her crew?" My brother was asking all of the damn questions today.

Now it was my turn to go mute. I, in fact, was in my woman's city, but there were no discussions nor plans of me meeting her parents or friends. I hadn't been entirely forthcoming with my brother about me and Jemma's situationship. While she was ready to be somebody's girlfriend, my lady was unprepared to expose our relationship.

Her parents were aware that she was in town; however, I honestly wasn't sure what she told them about where she'd been for the past week. Shit, I was unsure of what she shared about me if anything.

"Damn, Big. What are you? A private investigator," I scoffed.

"No. I won't be meeting her parents. We're not ready for that yet," I croaked because I did not believe the shit I was spewing.

"*We* or *she?*" Ezra said, refusing to back down.

"We, man, damn," I barked.

"Yeah, ok, Lil. Whatever you say? Let me go find something to eat. I'll holla at you later. Love you, bro," he muttered, ending the call before this conversation went downhill real fast.

"Alright. Love you, bro."

I leaned back against the headboard in our hotel suite, contemplating my brother's inquiries. That shit bothered me because it confirmed what I'd already been feeling. Jemma hadn't mentioned anything about connecting with her friends or even leaving the damn room for dinner. We'd spent the past two days in the suite.

I'd never spent extended time in St. Louis beyond a flight layover, so I wanted to explore the city a bit. Jemma's hesitance wasn't going to stop my show. I made plans that could include or *exclude* her. It would be her choice. Although St. Louis was much bigger than Monroe to hide in, masking *us* was not on my agenda.

"Hey," a sweet voice whispered.

I looked up from my phone and greeted her with the same smile she blessed me with.

Jemma was so damn graceful, even in casual jean shorts and a t-shirt. Her long braids were partially pulled into a ponytail, and gold hoop earrings grazed her shoulder. Her skin was still sunkissed from our time in Florida. She appeared rested and serene, my preferred version of my Jules.

"Hey. Did you have a good time?" I inquired, resting my phone on the nightstand.

"Yes. My line sisters are always a good time," she said, advancing into the room and climbing on the bed.

"What did you do today?" She kissed my bare stomach.

"Worked out," I responded, fondling through her braids.

"Ah, that's why you taste so salty," she giggled, softly biting into my flesh.

"Salty?" I responded questioningly. "Come here. Let me give you some of this saltiness," I joked, tickling her waist as I flipped her over.

I hovered, staring directly into that pretty, unblemished face.

"You don't see me complaining," she uttered, trailing pointy fingernails down my abs.

She bit the corner of her lip before filling my mouth with her tongue. Grabbing the back of my head, Jemma kissed me so hard and long that our lips were swollen. I loved it when she was the aggressor. An aggressive Jules meant that I could make love to her any way I desired... No limitations. I yearned to lick and lap her bodacious body from head to toe, but I had to get cleaned up first.

"Shower with me," I mumbled through a kiss as she sucked my bottom lip.

"My pleasure."

We kissed and caressed while undressing as we stumbled into the ensuite bathroom. Jemma used the restroom while I started the shower. I found some music to set the mood before laying my phone on the counter. Ginuwine "So Anxious" blared, and I caught a glimpse of my beam in the mirror. The song told no lies; I was so damn anxious... Fucking eager and impatient every time I had the opportunity to make love to Jules. I stepped into the shower to test the water temperature while I waited for her to join me.

"Hey, babe?" she rasped, getting my attention.

"Yeah, baby," I answered.

"Do you mind if I change the music?" she requested.

"Not at all. You know the code," I called from behind the shower door.

As the music momentarily paused, I perched on the marble bench allowing the steam to soothe my soreness. I wet my hands, then rubbed them down my face, growing impatient while waiting for her gorgeous body to grace me with its presence.

A familiar drum beat followed by soprano harmonies caused my brows to rise. Ludacris "Splash Waterfalls" echoed off the marble walls as Jemma's naked frame stepped into the shower with a swing to her hips, mouthing the words. *Make love to me. Fuck me.*

"Damn, Jules. That's what you're on, baby," I growled, absently stroking my dick.

She nodded, gorgeous honey orbs gazing at me with so much love and lust.

The steaming water pummeled our bodies as we continued to dissect each other with our tongues. Jemma felt so fucking good against my skin. The woman I met many months ago was uncertain and self-conscious about her scars, but the woman I was loving today unabashedly touched her breasts and fed me her nipples like I was a starving child.

I nipped, licked, and suckled her titties at a dragging frequency. Gliding my hands down her belly, I peeled back the plump folds of her pussy to reveal her swollen clit. I slowly circled two fingers against her bud while manipulating her nipples with the tip of my tongue.

Jules' eyes were sealed tight as she tossed her head back, digesting every morsel of gratifying sensation. I guided those same two fingers further down her slope and unhurriedly entered her essence. Traversing in and out and in and out, Jemma uncaged a violent moan.

She flopped on the shower seat, presumably needing a minute to recover, but my Jules shocked the shit out of me when she reached for my dick and ushered it into her mouth. In the seated position, she was at the perfect level to swallow my shit whole.

"Jemma Jule, goddamn," I declared through gritted teeth.

I wouldn't last long like this, and Jemma knew I wasn't a fan of quickies unless absolutely necessary. We had time, so I was going to take my time. The shit felt good as hell, but I had to back away from her. I almost burst when I saw the hungriness in her eyes when she licked her lips. *Shit!*

I swiftly lifted Jemma, mounting her body against the wall while simultaneously driving into her pussy at a merciless tempo. My cadence of choice today was two slow deep strokes, followed by a few hard pounds, concluding with a sluggish withdrawal, pausing to tickle her g-spot.

"Zeke, shit, baby. I want... I need to come. Please, Zee," she whined, prolonging the wail of my name.

I had a choice to grant her wish or stay swimming a bit longer. I chose the latter. Carrying Jemma from the shower wall to the bench, my hardness remained lodged in her soft spot. Thank goodness for the water temperature control because I needed to maintain the steaminess while I continued to passionately exploit her body.

While her inhibitions were non-existent, this was as good a time as any to execute my plan. I wanted to have dinner with my lady tonight. A table at the hotel's rooftop restaurant was reserved just for us.

I gradually slowed my momentum, sliding my manhood from her womanly essence.

"Zee, baby, don't stop. I'm almost there," she panted, reaching for me, attempting to guide me back into her folds.

I skimmed my dick up and down her lining but denied her penetration.

"Do something with me, Jules," I requested, teasing her pussy and driving her wild.

"Baby, shit. What?" she hissed.

I snickered because she was pissed. Jemma was at the edge of a destructive orgasm, and I vetoed every attempt she made to experience ecstasy.

"What?" I parroted, mimicking her attitude.

Pausing the motion to cease every carnal sensation, I questioned, "Who are you talking to like that?"

"I'm sorry, baby. Please. Please, Zee. I'll do anything," Jemma begged, and it turned me the hell on.

"Anything?" I inquired, nestling my dick in the crease of her ass.

Jemma released an exasperated breath.

"Yes, anything. Just give it to me," she moaned.

"Give you what, Jules?" I continued to tease with my words and my rod.

"Stop playing, Dr. Green. Give me that dick, shit."

I snickered while crashing back into her pussy. A millisecond was all it required for Jemma to howl every name and salutation that she could give me.

"Good fucking girl," I complimented, sprinkling kisses down the center of her back. "Now let me wash you up. You need to be ready in two hours. We have reservations on the rooftop."

"Ezekiel! No," she attempted to shout, but her drawl was sluggish.

"You said *anything*, Jules. Now chop chop," I laughed, smacking her ass twice.

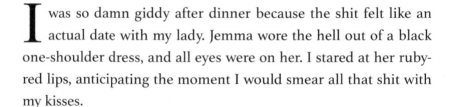

I was so damn giddy after dinner because the shit felt like an actual date with my lady. Jemma wore the hell out of a black one-shoulder dress, and all eyes were on her. I stared at her ruby-red lips, anticipating the moment I would smear all that shit with my kisses.

Jules nervously fingered the necklace that spelled *Jules* that I gifted her before we returned from vacation. The rooftop dinner event was small and intimate, so the chances of us running into someone she knew were slim. After a couple rounds of tequila and her favorite appetizers, she started to chill and enjoy the mellow atmosphere.

To my surprise, we even stayed a couple hours after dinner to listen to the live band. I wanted to stay longer, but when the tequila and cognac fully engaged, my and Jemma's hands started to roam. We were tipsy and horny, behaving like insatiable teenagers: dry humping on the elevator and fondling each other down the hall to our room. It was ridiculous but fun and sexy as hell.

When we entered the room, Jemma realized why I had declined dessert during our dinner. The balcony of our hotel was decorated with luminaries and roses. Coffee and gooey butter cake awaited us on a small table. Two chairs were not necessary because Jemma immediately sat on my lap. She fed me cake while we laughed and talked as she randomly licked powdered sugar from my face.

"Thank you, Zeke."

"For what, baby?" I questioned, wiping away the white residue from her lips.

"You always know what I need. You just keep showing up for me," she informed me before planting a sweet kiss on the tip of my nose.

"Every fucking time, Jemma."

I lost count of how many orgasms we were able to achieve when the night was over.

Jules

I thought I heard a phone ring in my dream, but when the blaring call sounded again, I knew I needed to wake up. I groaned, pissed that my deep slumber was being disrupted and my damn center was aching after last night's love-making marathon. I glanced at the illuminated screen to see it was almost one o'clock in the afternoon.

"Hey, Mama," I whispered. My voice was hoarse from the lack of sleep and screaming every version of Ezekiel's name half the night.

"Jemma Jule, what in the world is going on with you?" My mother's tone was loud and stern.

I grabbed my head, reeling from the Zeke and tequila-induced hangover. Sitting up straight in the bed that damn fast was a bad idea, but I felt like an adolescent being punished after missing curfew.

"What do you mean?" I probed, then my eyes popped open nervously.

Shit. Did somebody see us last night? I knew it was a bad idea.

"You've been back from wherever you were for three days and not once have you been over here to see your parents. Anything could be going on with us," Mama fussed.

"If something was going on, somebody would've called me by now, Mama."

"Don't sass me, lil girl. And have you talked to your daughter or are you ok with her galivanting across the wilderness with some boy?"

I rolled my eyes.

"Yes, I talked to Shiloh. And she's not galivanting or whatever. She's on a hiking trip sponsored by the university."

"With a boy she calls her boyfriend."

"Mama, she's fine. What's really going on? Why are you yelling?"

I gasped from the sensation of warm, acquainted hands being wrapped around my waist. He lifted a brow, and I mouthed, '*my mother.*' Zeke nodded, then pulled me into his stately yet comforting frame.

"I would just like to see my only child, that's all." My mother continued, but I almost forgot she was on the phone when he started kissing and licking my neck. "I don't believe that is too much to ask."

"No. No ma'am, it's not," I practically panted.

"Fine. Dinner will be ready at six. I'll see you then."

Before I could protest, she ended the call. I rolled my eyes, snuggling deeper into this chocolate-coated God.

"You good?" Ezekiel questioned, kneading at the small of my back.

"Yeah. Just my mother complaining about not seeing me."

"You *have* been here a few days, babe. Are you hiding, Jules? Hiding me?" he asked while faintly brushing his lips against my shoulder.

I turned my body towards him and leered.

"Hiding. Why would I need to hide? I wasn't *hiding* us last night," I said with an attitude.

"Yeah, but you weren't completely comfortable initially. Once you confirmed that you didn't know anyone, you started to relax."

I rolled my eyes and pulled the covers over my breast. I was pouting like a little ass girl because he was right.

Ezekiel snickered, biting into his bottom lip.

"Why are you getting upset?" He flicked the tip of my nose, and I swatted his hand away.

"I know you, sweetheart. You get defensive when you refuse to admit that I'm right."

"I'm not... I'm not hiding, Zeke. I just don't know what to do and I don't want to disappoint anybody any more than I already have."

"How have you been a disappointment, Jules?" He nudged my chin, lifting it to make eye contact.

"The demise of me and Quinton. Quinton with a baby. His cheating and my ignoring it. Shiloh's falling apart. And I'm afraid to admit-" I swallowed hard. My words were lodged in my throat.

"Afraid to admit what, babe? Talk to me," he uttered.

"That the only time I feel whole and authentic... is when I'm with you. And it's not fair to you that I can't share my joy. I can't share *you*, Zee," I croaked every word because I genuinely didn't know how he would respond.

Zeke

"It's not fair to you, Jemma." I stressed. "You should be able to live your life the way that you choose but-" I halted, pinching the bridge of my nose because I didn't want to hurt her feelings.

"What?" Jemma sat up in the bed, covering her breasts with the sheet.

"You have to stop worrying about what people are going to think. Do what the fuck makes you happy, Jules. If that's me, great. Shit, I'm winning. If it's not, that'll break my fucking heart... but so be it because all I desire is that you are happy." I pulled her into me, forcing eye contact. "What does your heart need, baby? I know your daughter is always the number one priority, but once she's good, what about you? Hmm?"

Jemma chewed her bottom lip as tears streamed down her face. She spent so much time worrying about what everybody else wanted that she rarely did something for Jemma without looking over her shoulder to see who could be watching. Who was whispering behind her back.

Last night's dinner was a test. If she would've refused, I had a backup plan for dinner in our suite. But I wanted to demonstrate to her that we could be together publicly and the world would not crumble.

"My heart wants to be..." She huffed, unable to complete the sentence.

"Use your words." I encouraged her, stroking my knuckle down her cheek.

"Free. I want to *truly* be free, Zeke. I carry so much guilt when I know deep down this was not my fault. But I still feel responsible, ya know. Like I have to clean up the mess. Be perfect, unblemished Dr. Jemma Holiday, even if it is a facade."

I shook my head and rubbed a hand down my face. Sitting up in bed, I looked back at her. Her tears broke and enraged my heart at the same damn time. I never wanted to see Jules shed a tear, but it pissed me off that she still didn't comprehend her strength.

"A facade? That's not the Jemma Jule Holiday I know. The woman I met at that restaurant almost ten months ago was a boss. She stepped out of her comfort zone to have her first one night stand," I praised, allowing a lust-filled grin to grace my face.

She blushed, seemingly reminiscing on the first night we met in Monroe City when we talked, drank, and laughed until we fell asleep, designating it as the one-night stand of our dreams.

"Nobody is saying that you have to make a grand announcement about whatever it is we're doing, but..." I deliberated my next words as she glared at me with misty eyes.

"I *won't* be a secret, Jemma. In this situationship, we do what's convenient for your circumstance. We're in a city that I've never visited, your hometown, and I don't get to experience it with the only person I want to be with. But I acquiesce, I go with your flow because I love *you,* Jules. But after last night... After the opportunity to gaze into those pretty eyes, enjoy dinner together, and smirk at the thirsty niggas ogling *my lady's* ass in that sexy black dress. Shit, that felt amazing and now I'm a greedy mutherfucka because I want more." I rose to my full height because I wanted to be done talking about this shit.

"Situationship? Really?" Jemma interrogated with a scowl.

"Yeah, situationship," I spat. "I'm not meeting your family. Your daughter walks right by me and has no clue I'm *mommy's boyfriend.* We can't even have a working lunch together without your head on a swivel."

I broke. I'd been holding this shit in for a minute, and the dam finally burst. When I confessed to Jemma that I loved her more than she could imagine, that shit was true. There was no confusion in my heart or my head. This woman had infiltrated the inner mechanics of my soul, and I was hooked. I was married for seventeen years and never realized this kind of love, intimacy, and friendship.

She'd become the rhythm that made my heart beat in such a short time. Jemma wasn't just a pretty face. She was one of the sexiest, witty, intelligent, comical, whimsical women I'd ever encountered. We could laugh for hours at old Richard Pryor comedy albums while at the same time debating the need for better reproductive rights. My Jules was a fucking stunner, a rare find. And goddammit, I wanted her... *every fucking time.*

6

JULES

I hopped in the shower to get dressed for dinner with my parents. Although dinner was at six, my mother called, asking me to stop at the store for strawberries for her pound cake and Pepsi for my daddy. With downtown traffic, I needed to leave earlier than planned.

Ezekiel left a few minutes ago to exercise in the hotel's gym. He mentioned he may go for a run if it wasn't too hot. I shook my head, recalling the hurt and vexation on his face when he kissed my forehead, nose, and lips before he darted out of the door.

When I awakened this morning, I had no dream that Zeke and I would experience our first fight as a... *situationship*. I don't know why that title pissed me off. It was so unemotional and dispassionate, the complete opposite of *us*. But sadly, he was right. While our connection was bigger than Jupiter, our courtship dwelled in a contained box. Incapable of growing and flourishing... because of *me*.

I huffed, trying to find something comfortable to wear because I was in a mood. Opting for a sleeveless knit jumper, I tossed my braids into a ponytail, slapped some Vaseline on my lips, and that was all the effort I had for the day.

Zeke had not returned, and I needed to leave. I tried calling him, but I believed this man was sending me to voicemail. After my third call, he sent me a voice message saying, *"I'm running. Enjoy your dinner."*

I responded with a voice message of my own.

"Hey babe, I need to leave a few minutes earlier than planned. My mom needs me to pick up a few things from the store. I was hoping you could be back so we could talk. But..." I sighed. *"Look, Zeke, I'm sorry. I know that this is not an ideal situation, but I want to figure this out."*

I paused for a long minute. So long that I exhausted the maximum time for the recording. I left a second message.

"I'm not sure what you've planned for dinner, but my Mama is a really good cook. I'll, um, I'll bring you a plate."

I slapped my forehead to my palm, irritated at myself because I sounded foolish.

I pulled into my parents' driveway after stopping at the local grocery store to pick up my mother's requested items. Checking my phone, I sighed because Ezekiel had not responded to my voicemail, and I didn't blame him. As our relationship progressed, things just seemed more complex.

The choice to love Zeke was easy because he made it so. However, integrating him into my complications was an entirely different scenario. While I experienced the nurturing and beauty of the man, I wasn't sure what others would see. Sighing, I pressed to code to open the garage and entered my childhood home.

"Hey, hey," I hailed while holding the bags and closing the door with my foot.

"Hey, hey," my dad retorted. "Why didn't you call me to come and get the bags?" Daddy questioned, relinquishing the light load as he kissed my cheek.

"It's not too heavy, daddy," I replied, walking over to my mother at the sink to place a kiss on her cheek.

"Hi, Mama."

"Well, hello, my heart. Dinner will be ready in a few. Put those rolls in the oven for me please," Mama directed.

I nodded.

"Is it just us?" I asked, neatly lining the dinner rolls on the baking sheet.

"Child, yes. I wasn't in the mood for company today. Your father has been mister entertainment lately so I just wanted some quiet time for us to catch up."

I knew exactly what that meant. My mother, also known as inspector gadget, was about to play a game of clue to determine what her daughter had been up to lately. I hadn't necessarily lied to my mother about my whereabouts the past couple of weeks; I just omitted *him*.

"Uh oh. Mauri is ready to catch up, Jem. You know what that means, babygirl," daddy quipped.

"Oh, whatever, Gavin," Mama said, tossing her hand at my father when he swatted her butt.

I shook my head, laughing. My parents had always exemplified the love I aspired to experience. Gavin Warren and Maureen Floyd met and fell in love the summer before my mother's freshman year at Monroe University. Daddy was a new student orientation leader, and mom was attending a summer program for presidential scholars. The way my father tells the story, he fell in love at first sight with a pretty cinnamon-hued girl with sandy-brown ringlets hanging from her ponytail, eager to learn everything about the university. They married while my father was in medical school, shortly after my mother graduated with her undergraduate degree. Almost immediately after they said, "I do," I was born. Dr. and Mrs. Gavin Warren epitomized regalness, respect, and adoration.

"Jemma Jule. Dinner," Mama called my name in a way that only she could.

Dinner was displayed across the dining room table as if an army was being fed. My mother was definitely on a mission because she cooked my favorites. Creamy roasted chicken, mashed potatoes, corn, and sriracha brussel sprouts. She even made a pineapple cheesecake. My mother plated my father's food before fixing her own. I glared at my phone again, hoping Zeke would have responded by now.

"How was your trip, honey?" my dad asked, disrupting my fruitless stare at my phone.

"It was good. Very relaxing," I replied, fingering the necklace Ezekiel gifted me.

"Well, where did you go?" Mama inquired while scooping a helping of potatoes into her mouth.

"Mama, I told you I was going to Florida." I wanted to roll my eyes, but Maureen Warren would still pop me in my mouth at forty years old.

"Alone?" Mama asked, tone dripping with doubt. "Because Quaron and Maxine were in New York," she continued to probe.

"I took a trip, Mama. A well-deserved trip to a beautiful beach in Florida like I told you before."

"I don't understand why it has to be such a secret, Jemma," she blurted with an attitude.

I glared at my mother, but all I could hear was Ezekiel's declaration. *I won't be a secret, Jemma.*

I huffed, dropping my fork, causing it to loudly clap against the plate. My mother and I were involved in an intense eye war at this point. I wiped the corners of my mouth with the cloth napkin, then tossed it on the table.

"Ok, fine. You want to know, Mama? I went to Florida with a man that I have been seeing recently. The trip was wonderful. *He* is wonderful and is becoming pretty important to me, and -"

"Jemma Jule," my mother scoffed, interrupting me. "Do you call yourself being in love, little girl? The ink is barely dry on the divorce papers."

"Mauri!" my father yelped, giving my mother a gentle warning.

"Gavin! Do you hear your daughter? She was married for twenty years, gets a divorce practically overnight, and now she's *dating,*" my mother verbalized, with disgust wrinkling her beautiful face. "Shiloh is falling apart and you have time to *date.*" Mama readjusted her wrath back to me.

Tears welled in my eyes, not from hurt but from anger. I loved my mother dearly. She was my first best friend... But often a *judgmental* best friend. While I was the apple of her eye, the perfectionist in me was siphoned directly from the DNA of Maureen Warren. Every speech, every dance recital, and every report card had to be flawless. Not one hair could be out of place... no exceptions.

I can still remember the disappointment creasing the corners of her earthy brown eyes when I mumbled the words, '*I'm pregnant.*' The way she barked, '*Jemma Jule, how could you do this to me?*' shattered my heart.

My mother was my nucleus, the core of my soul. Disappointing her was never an option. I'd spent the past twenty years making amends for my blunder. The best student, best wife, best mom, best administrator, best writer, and best friend. I was *exhausted.*

But what about being the best girlfriend to Zeke? I thought. A man who saw allure and grace in my every imperfection.

"Jemma, sweetheart. What's going on, honey?" My mother's tone softened.

"Maybe this is a rebound, Maureen. Nothing is wrong with that after the hell she's been through," my daddy spoke.

He and my mother went back and forth for what felt like an eternity as I just sat there. Placid. Affected but unmoved. I huffed with my eyes sealed tight. Deeply inhaling, then exhaling, I slowly opened my eyes to look at my parents.

What does your heart need, baby? I pondered Zeke's question, wishing I could cradle in his protective hold right now.

"Shiloh has always been and will always be my first priority without question," I finally spoke, disrupting their bickering. "First and foremost, I want to be very clear about that. I am a good mother," I cried, but my tenor was steadfast.

"But Shiloh is twenty years old and the one thing I always taught her is that life is going to happen, regardless of the plans you've made or your preferences. And now she's experiencing the hard stuff that comes with living *life*. And I will be there to help her navigate every peak and valley." I paused, standing from my seat at the dinner table.

"As for what's going on with me... I too am experiencing life. I've been a mother and a wife since I was twenty years old. I am a different woman now. What I needed then versus what my heart desires today has changed. I'm also on a journey to figure out what's best for Jemma. My peace... my freedom." *My Zee.*

I didn't lend sound to my last words as I walked away, fumbling with my phone, trying to navigate to Ezekiel's contact. With blurred vision and a heavy heart, I typed what I was certain was gibberish, carefully climbing the steps to my childhood room. I snickered because even at forty years old, I was hesitant to lock my bedroom door in my parents' house. Collapsing across my bed, I cried myself into an unexpected slumber.

"Jemma Jule," my mother's melodic timbre hailed from downstairs.

After all of this time, I still immediately awakened at the sound of her voice. I reluctantly schlepped out of my bed and opened the door. I heard muffled dialogue at the front door while my mother's petite frame was leaning against the wooden stair post with her arms crossed, staring up at me.

"Yes, Mama," I inquired, rubbing my tired, dry eyes.

She did not speak a word, just shifted her leer towards the front door. Unhurriedly taking one step at a time, I wanted to jump the remaining steps when the milk chocolate-hued God came into my view.

Zee.

My father scratched his brow, obviously skittish and confused.

"Um, Jemma, Dr. Green says he's here to see you. And I don't believe this is official university business," Daddy said, vainly attempting to minimize the amusement in his voice.

He winked at me, then stepped aside to allow Ezekiel to enter the house.

Zeke peered at me, unsuccessfully subduing the smile curving his lips. Powder blue never looked so sexy on a man. Everything about his dominant, confident posture wreaked *I'm coming for you every fucking time.*

"Jemma, do you care to explain?" Mama asked, her hands resting on the ample hips she gifted me. "Why is the *Provost* of Monroe University here to see you?"

I pinched my lips, trying my damndest to quell the beam growing on my face. Clearly, I dropped my location to Zeke when I thought I was texting him because here he was. Every damn time I needed him.

"Because... Dr. Green ... Um, Ezekiel is the man I was referring to."

"The rebound?" My mother sneered.

"Maureen! Now that's enough." My father sternly warned, causing Mama to toss up her hands in surrender.

Ezekiel's eyes narrowed. Her accusation troubled him, but he never disjoined his stare from me.

"No Mama. He's not a rebound," I clarified, hastening to abbreviate any more time away from him.

I beheld his gaze, feeling the heated intensity of this moment seep from our pores.

"Jemma, answer me," Mama called from behind me, seeking an explanation.

"He's my boyfriend." I smiled.

Ezekiel blessed me with that Colgate-white smile I could now admit I fell in love with at first sight. He swiped a fingertip down the slope of my nose before gently pinching my chin.

"You came," I rasped.

"Every time."

7

JULES

A week had zoomed by since my *boyfriend* met my parents. Ezekiel awkwardly stood in the doorway for at least five more minutes before my father offered him dinner. The invitation was met with a stern apprehensive leer from my mother. I sat beside him and couldn't digest a morsel of my unfinished plate because my heart was stuck in my damn right toe. I was like a teenage girl whose boyfriend was meeting her parents for the first time.

My mother retreated to the kitchen, and I joined her since my father, and Zeke were intently discussing golf and politics. The honey eyes that I'd admired all of my life were saddened. My mother was grieving. She lost a son in Quinton, and in some ways, she lost the old Jemma.

The divorce had changed things for everyone. I battled between guilt and gladness, feeling the impact of my mother's melancholy. At the same time, Ezekiel's laugh echoing from the dining room caused a bliss that I couldn't explain.

I stood next to her at the kitchen sink and began to rinse the dishes as she washed. Mama and I were similar in many ways, so I knew I needed to give her an opportunity to speak her peace. Release whatever hurt she was holding.

"This is hard, Jemma. For twenty years, we've been a family. A unit. And now -" Mama shook her head, seemingly in disbelief about our new normal. "I just don't want you to be hurt anymore, babygirl. I'm worried about you. I'm worried about Shiloh. Dammit, I'm even worried about Quinton's ass," Mama chuckled through a cry.

"But this," she whispered, pointing toward the dining room. "It's too much, too fast. He's too much. A blind woman can see why you're smitten with that man, but a boyfriend, Jemma? The university provost? It just sounds plain crazy. A scandal. What will people think? What does Shiloh have to say about this? She should be your priority. As parents, sometimes we have to put our needs on the backburner. And I believe this is one of those times, sweetheart."

My phone chimed through the car speaker, saving me from the continued replay of the conversation with my mother.

Quinton: In traffic. Five minutes late.

I responded *ok*, then checked myself in the rearview mirror. I was sitting in the parking lot of Dr. Ray's office. Since Quinton and Shiloh were going to be a few minutes late, I decided to head into the office and get us checked in.

My phone rang just as I was about to exit the car. His handsome face was exactly what I didn't realize I needed at the moment.

"Hey," I greeted him with almost too much cheer in my voice.

"Hey, beautiful. I just wanted to give you a quick call to let you know I'm thinking about you," Zeke announced.

"Thank you. I needed that." I sighed, allowing the hush to linger.

"You ok," he said questioningly.

"Yeah, just a little nervous."

"What did I tell you last night, baby?" he said, staring directly into the camera at me.

"Before or after you put a spell on my pussy?" I teased.

Zeke boisterously laughed. "Before," he quipped, then winked.

"To listen to Shiloh *and her dad*," I scoffed, rolling my eyes as he continued to chuckle.

"Yes, and to speak your truth. Share what your heart needs too, Jemma. Everyone should have the opportunity to speak their truth, pain, and what they need to heal," Zeke advised.

"I hear you, babe."

"Alright. Let me get to this meeting so I can finish packing. I'll see you later," he vowed, giving me the sexiest, most supportive gaze.

I nodded. "Yes. Later. Bye, Zeke."

"Good afternoon, Ms. Holiday." The receptionist greeted me.

"Good afternoon."

"Dr. Ray said you can go on in. I will send in your daughter and Mr. Holiday when they arrive," she instructed.

I thanked her and then walked into the office I'd become very familiar with over the past several months. Dr. Ray assisted me in navigating one of the most tumultuous times of my life. I prayed that he could help my daughter out of the dark hole she had entered in recent months.

My Shi had not been herself since discovering her father's infidelity, resulting in a child and divorce. She began showing signs of depression, and Quinton and I were terrified. Her grades started slipping, and she quit track and completely retreated to her dorm. Initially, she had only disregarded Quinton, but now the entire family was beginning to feel the cold shoulder, especially me.

Shiloh had never been a disrespectful child, but her bad attitude and smart mouth were getting out of hand. A few weeks ago, I recommended she start seeing Dr. Ray because otherwise, I would likely knock her teeth down her throat. I empathized with her but would not tolerate rude behavior or defiance towards me or her father.

Dr. Ray requested that we consider family sessions, so here we were. This was the first meeting, and I had to admit I was angsty and honestly did not know what to expect. I prayed this shit didn't turn into an episode of the real housewife of *Monroe City*.

"Knock, knock. Hey, Dr. Ray. Is it ok to come in?" I sang.

"Yes, Jemma. Hello. Come on in," his melodic, soothing voice rang.

"How have you been?" I asked, taking a seat at the end of the leather couch.

"Doing very well. Thank you. How was your vacation?" he asked, standing from his desk to sit across from me.

"It was wonderful." The sparkle in my tenor couldn't be denied.

"I see," Dr. Ray said with a slight smile. "You're glowing."

"I am," I confidently declared, one hundred percent agreeing with his observation.

"We'll dig into that during our session next week, yes?"

I nodded.

Dr. Ray and I engaged in small talk while we waited. About ten minutes later, Quinton leisurely strolled into the room dressed in slacks and a dress shirt rolled up to his elbows. The only time this man rushed to do anything was in a competitive race. I glanced at the door expecting Shiloh to walk in behind him with the same casual pace. The crease in my brow voiced my hushed words.

"She's in the restroom. She's also in a mood," he sneered, occupying the space on the opposite end of the couch.

"Hello, Mr. Holiday. It's good to meet you," Dr. Ray spoke as he witnessed our exchange.

"Dr. Ray, my apologies. Hello. It's nice to meet you." Quinton stood to shake his hand.

At that moment, it occurred to me that this *was* Quinton's first time meeting the therapist since he never attended a couple's therapy session.

Shiloh trudged into the office, looking as if she just rolled out of bed. Dressed in track shorts, a wrinkled university t-shirt, and slides with her hair pulled into a messy bun, I was appalled at her appearance. This was not my Shiloh.

"Hi, Shi," I muttered, eyeing her from head to toe as she stepped over my feet.

She sat between me and Quinton and leaned over to kiss me on my cheek.

"Hey, Mommy," she whispered, then crossed her arms.

Lord, give me strength.

I glanced down the couch to Quinton, and he appeared to be lifting up a similar prayer.

"Hello, Shiloh," Dr. Ray greeted her.

"Hi, Dr. Ray." A faint smile slanted her lips.

Dr. Ray spent the next several minutes setting expectations for our next ninety minutes together. He encouraged both Quinton and me to listen without speaking or anticipation. He gave us a pad of paper to write down any clarifying questions. We nodded in agreement to his directives.

"Mr. Holiday, Shiloh has shared a lot with me about your relationship and I've asked her to express how she feels to you. Before she begins, once again, I need you to remember your commitment to simply listening. Her words may sting, but right now, she does not need a retort or reaction."

Quinton nodded.

Dr. Ray signaled for Shiloh to speak when she was ready.

She released an exasperated breath before she said, "Daddy, I want to hate you."

Oh shit! I quietly mused.

"Since the day you admitted to cheating on mommy and getting a woman pregnant, I've wanted to hate you. All of my life you've been my hero, my superman. Every boy I've ever liked, I compared to my daddy because you loved mommy and loved me without effort. So that day when my world changed forever, I felt like you didn't only cheat on mommy, you cheated on me." Shiloh's face was drenched with tears.

I watched Quinton, and his heart broke a little more with every word. Thumbing away a stray tear, it was my instinct to support my babygirl through this. I rested my hand atop Shiloh's, and she immediately clasped her hand in mine as she continued.

"One of the worst days of my life as a daddy's girl was when I realized that my Superman, my hero, is merely just a man. You broke my heart, daddy," Shiloh croaked.

Her face collapsed into the palms of her hands as she explosively wailed. Quinton was desperate to comfort her, but Dr. Ray shook his head, instructing him to wait. The silence hovered over us like a dark cloud, ready to wreak havoc.

"I'm hurt. I'm angry. I'm confused," she blurted.

"By what, Shiloh? Tell *both* of your parents why you're hurt, angry, and confused," Dr. Ray coached.

"He has a baby. My... *sister,*" Shiloh scoffed, directing her attention to the therapist.

"Do you expect me to accept a sister that destroyed my family?" she said, now focusing her question on Quinton.

Not leaving room to breathe, she quickly shifted her body to face me.

"Mommy, you said we were going to be OK. But I'm *not* OK. You're dating and it's like you've just moved on... from everything. From me."

"Shi-" I disregarded the doctor's directions and tried to interject. I wanted to console my child.

Dr. Ray lifted one finger, silencing me immediately.

"I've seen you with him, mommy. Dr. Green. Yeah, I know he's more than just your friend. I've seen him leaving your house," Shiloh spat, then resumed her indignant stance as she faced the doctor.

Oh shit, I pondered again, but I actually think I whispered the words.

"So basically, my daddy is somebody else's daddy, and my mother is dating the provost of my school. It's embarrassing. I see people whispering... Looking at me, *laughing* at me. What the hell do you want me to do with this? I don't know this life," Shiloh shouted.

Her piercing screech was drenched with misery and dejection. I couldn't breathe, and I felt the moment when Quinton lost his air too. The one alliance Quinton and I maintained was Shiloh; now we'd broken her heart. I prayed that we hadn't destroyed her life.

"Shiloh, what do you want to happen with all of this?" Dr. Ray's tenor was gentle, acknowledging my daughter's fragile state.

"I - I want my family back."

8

JULES

I had no clue how I made it home in one piece. My eyes burned from hot tears that wouldn't cease as I drove from Dr. Ray's office. I guess because I was carrying precious cargo: my Shiloh. She wanted to come home with me tonight, and of course, I didn't hesitate. I wish I could have scooped my baby girl up in my arms and assured her that it was going to be OK. But it was not going to be OK. I was willing to give my life for my daughter, cut the heart of my chest if she needed it. But a family dynamic between me and her dad would never happen again. I couldn't grant that wish for her. Quinton and I would always be a team for the sake of Shi but never husband and wife.

At Shiloh's request, we stopped to pick up ice cream before ordering food from her favorite spot for wings. We rode in silence other than the periodic chime of my phone. I knew that it was Ezekiel, but I could not disrupt this time with Shiloh. She'd actually opened up, and I did not want to hinder that. Releasing an exasperated breath, I reluctantly silenced his attempt for at least the fourth time.

Shiloh's breakdown was my demise. I felt like the stretchy guy from The *Fantastic Four*, being pulled in every direction. The only problem was I wasn't a scientific mishap with the ability to stretch, twist, and contour my body beyond human proportions. I was merely a mom, a woman who was utterly fatigued by being *somebody* to everybody else.

Once Shiloh and I ate and chatted more, she retired to her room and immediately fell asleep. I schlepped to the kitchen for what would be my third glass of wine. Lifting the bottle, there was just a drop left. I shrugged, then turned up the empty bottle and stuck my tongue out to ensure I could get the last dollop. An eerie chuckle escaped my lungs, sounding like a combination of a scornful sneer and an agonizing sob.

I settled in my sunroom, staring at the rose bush as my tears continued to fall. I traced the outline of the yellow roses at least a thousand times. I was in a trance. Visions of Shiloh's frantic disposition spilling her truth replayed in my head like the skip of a record.

Why did this have to be so hard? I just wanted to be a woman who loved a new man... Without shame or family obligation. I had ample time to cry and process the stages of grief over the past year due to the dissolution of my marriage, but my family had not. While I was basking in the sea of acceptance and hope, their grief was new, causing them to wade in the waters of anger and depression.

Hearing heavy footsteps padding through my house quickly deepened my reality. I closed my eyes and audibly exhaled because it was *him*. His tall, imposing frame reflected in the glass of the patio doors as he slowly ambled, searching for me. I eyed his confused countenance as he gawked at the unpacked suitcase and clothes sprawled over the couch. Ezekiel advanced towards the sunroom; familiar with my routine when distressed, he knew exactly where to find me.

"Jules." His voice was throaty. He was worried. "Baby, I've been calling you. Are you OK?"

I shook my head, then cradled my knees into my body.

"Jemma, what happened?" Ezekiel asked as he rounded the chair to stand in front of me.

"Shiloh," I cried.

He knelt before me and unlocked my tense legs.

"What do you mean? Is she OK? Is she hurt?" he probed, anticipatory.

"She's asleep, but she's *not* OK." I shrugged.

"Do you want to talk about it?" He stroked the top of my hand while kissing my thumb.

"No. But I know we need to," I stood to close the door.

Shiloh didn't need to be privy to the conversation. I absolutely detested this chat, but there was a big ass elephant in the room that needed to be addressed.

Zeke now occupied the chair I was sitting in. He took my hand and guided me to sit on his lap. Resting my head on his shoulder, I remained mute for what felt like a lifetime, but only a few heartbeats drummed.

"I can't go to New York, Zee," I murmured, sniffing back the impairing emotions.

"I figured that much. I'll reschedule with the resort. You can come when Shiloh is settled."

"No. Babe, I, um... I need to focus on Shiloh. For as long as it takes," I pledged, trembling.

"What are you saying, Jemma?" he interrogated me, brow crumpled in uncertainty.

He cupped my chin in his hand and forced me to look at him. Tears flooded my eyes at the thought of any amount of separation from this man. But I had to do what was best for Shiloh. Like my mother said, I had to put my needs on the back burner.

Clearing my throat while aggressively wiping my eyes, I blurted, "Dr. Green, I think we need to take a break."

Ezekiel eerily snickered, shaking his head. "Dr. Green," he mumbled slowly. "We're back to the formalities?"

I shook my head and held my breath, attempting to stop my sobs. The kiss on my temple instigated the torrential waters that leaked from my eyes.

"Those tears, the look on your face... They don't match breaks, Jules, or goodbyes." He kissed my face everywhere.

"Zeke, Shiloh is falling apart and I have to do everything in my power to help her," I explained, desperate for him to comprehend.

"I understand that, Jemma. I would never ask you not to prioritize your daughter. But... A break, baby?" he rasped, swallowing hard to seemingly clear the boulder stuck in his throat.

"A break," he repeated, scowling as if the words tasted like shit. "How long?" he enquired through gritted teeth.

I shrugged, but my dismissive behavior conflicted with the commotion stirring in my chest.

"Use your words, wordsmith," he stated harshly, and I don't believe he gave a damn.

"I don't know. I don't know. Until we -"

"Until what?" Zeke interrupted. "Until you and her father make it work? Because I'm sure that's what she wants, right? You know how I know? Because that is exactly what EJ and Eriya wanted for me and their mother. But that is not what was best for any of us. Is that what's best for you, Jemma?"

"Ezekiel, you know it's not," I whined.

"This conversation is showing me that I really don't know shit," he scoffed.

The bitter chuckle carried no humor at all. Lifting me from his lap, Zeke stood, opening the sliding door. He slowly paced into the house with his hands resting on his nape.

I followed behind him as he continued his prowling motion. He aimlessly roved while I unconsciously retreated.

"I told you I was going to be fucked up over this. And here we are. I'm not going to be the rebound and damn sure won't continue to operate in the background, Jemma," he uttered, and his tenor was cold.

Despite Ezekiel's closed expression, I could sense his vulnerability... his angst. He glared at me with narrowed eyes, questions, and ambivalence circling in his gaze. Under his scrutiny, I grew more unresolved and was unraveling by the minute. He approached me with a powerful, stealthy stride, so my feet paddled backward until he pinned me against the wall. His imposition was menacing, but the dew clouding his eyes straddled between love and heart-wrenching pain.

Zeke seized my entire face into the palms of his hands before he whispered against my lips, "No. No breaks."

"Just some time, Zee. So I can figure this out." I pleaded, kissing his palms, his fingertips, anything that allowed me to maintain a connection with him.

He closed his eyes and shook his head. Ezekiel released from my hold, and my body went limp, uncontrollably sliding down my living room wall.

"Nah, then what? You figure this out, then there's something else. Somebody else who's not pleased," he assured, kneeling in front of me.

He kissed against my knee, then straightened my legs to rest atop his. Pulling my body to straddle him, Zeke's kisses were so tender, nourishing my every need.

"What about what you desire, Jules? What about your heart?

What about me, baby?" he muttered, swirling his tongue in that one salacious spot on my neck.

"Zee," I whimpered. Shit practically moaned.

"Do I need to fuck some sense into you, baby? Can I love this *break* bullshit away? Hmm, Jules," he whispered.

Ezekiel glided his tongue down my clavicle and settled in my cleavage. His massive hands caressed my swollen breasts through the thin fabric of my tank top. He paid special attention to my nipples, that instantly swelled in response to his touch.

"Just give me some time. Please. I promise I'll come to you. When I fix this, I will be there every time, babe."

I retreated because I knew that any form of separation would be non-existent if this man entered any of my orifices. But I had to consider Shiloh. I had no other choice. We coupled our foreheads and interchanged pained breaths.

"I love you, Jemma Jule. I'm still working my ass off to mend everything that's been broken in you. I still have so much work to do, baby. I'm not done yet. Let me finish. Please," he begged, and it broke my fucking heart.

We cradled in silence, vying for space to exhale. My body tingled from the closeness, our silent intimacy. Anybody watching would assume this was a peaceful encounter, but the turmoil racing through our hearts was chaotic.

"But a break, Jules. Nah... This sounds like *the end*. The end before it even fucking starts," he sighed, the beautiful milk chocolate hue of his skin slowly drained.

"This is not the end. This can't be the end. Zee, I love you."

Zeke sprinkled kisses on my forehead.

"Zee," I called through muffled cries as vehement tears saturated his skin.

"I pray everything works out for Shiloh. And for you, Jules. If you need me, you know what to do, right?"

I nodded.

"I love you, Zeke."

"Jules, baby. I love you more than you'll ever know."

~

I squinted, shielding my eyes from the disgruntled sun rays shining in my living room. The wall of windows was my favorite part of this house, but on this particular morning, I despised the luminous glare. Cradled on the couch, I immediately regretted shifting positions because my head was banging. The alcohol, crying, and missing Ezekiel-induced hangover won the war I didn't even know I was fighting.

The incessant buzzing of my phone withdrew me from my sleep. I ignored it for as long as possible because I knew it wasn't Ezekiel. Maxine and Quaron's unique tone sounded again. I stretched, looking around for my phone, which wasn't readily visible. My friends would not stop calling, and the sound was driving me crazy. I finally found my phone buried in the couch cushion.

Maxi: Jemma, are you ok? I've been calling you.

Roni: Jem, are you seriously not coming to New York? I just talked to Ez.

Maxi: Wait, what? Why not?

Roni: I love my niece, but come on, you gotta live too.

Maxi: Stop talking in code. What the hell happened? I'm on my way.

I called them instead of responding to the text messages because if Max said she was on her way, she was likely halfway to the car.

"Maxi, you don't need to come. I'm ok." I lied, voice throaty.

"No you're not. You sound horrible. What happened?" Maxi demanded.

"I really don't feel like going into this right now, but Ezekiel and I are going to take a break from this... whatever it is," I spewed, and it actually did taste like shit.

"A break? That's bullshit," Quaron shouted.

"Jem, is that what you really want?" Maxine asked. Her voice was so delicate and soft.

I shook my head as if they could see me. Tears cascaded down my face, and I did not bother to clear them. Repeated sniffs were the only sounds I could produce.

I absently stared at the spot on the floor Zeke and I occupied for hours last night. He snugly cradled me until I cried myself to sleep. I abruptly woke up on the couch in the middle of the night, searching for him, but he was gone.

"The one time I want something just for me, I can't have it. While having him makes me happy, it hurts my Shi."

"J, I love my brother and I love my niece, but this is *not* OK. It's not fair that you have to choose. That you have to endure hurt to heal them... her," Roni fussed.

"Mommy."

Shiloh's groggy whisper and soft tap on my shoulder from behind the couch pulled me from my reverie. I swiped a lone tear and smiled at her.

"Are you OK?" she asked, concern lacing her pretty face.

"Hey, y'all. I need to go. I'll call you later," I ended the call.

"Yeah, Shi, I'm good. How are you, babygirl?" I inquired, tapping the seat next to me.

The fake smile I plastered on my face actually ached.

"How did you sleep?" I asked, swiping a curly tendril from her face.

"I slept OK. Did you sleep out here?" she asked, her brow furrowed as she looked around at the crumbled blankets.

I nodded.

"I guess I fell asleep on the couch." I lied again.

"What happened to New York? Shouldn't you be gone by now?" Shiloh probed with a bit of a scornful demeanor.

The look on her face actually confused me. I could not discern if she was happy, sad, or indifferent. It was an unusual combination of all three sentiments.

"I'm not going. I told you yesterday that I was here for whatever you needed. I am going to see you through this, Shi. I want you to be OK. I want *us* to be OK, babygirl."

Silence. Shiloh reacted with nothing but silence while she blankly stared out of the window at the garden. She appeared to be circling the lines of the rose bushes just as I did last night. Heeding Dr. Ray's advice, I gave my daughter the space and stillness to process her feelings.

"How can you still be around daddy and listen to him talk about what he's done? His *daughter*," she sneered, rolling her eyes before she continued. "... Without strangling him." Shi dropped her head back, eyes focused on the ceiling.

I mimicked her stance, clasping her hand as we both glared mutedly.

Sighing, I said, "Honestly, I don't know, Shi. Initially, I wanted to take his damn head off," I snickered. "But I considered you. I considered me and I even considered daddy. He made a mistake, babygirl. A big damn mistake, and it hurts, but nobody died. We live to breathe another day and try to do better. To be better."

"Why is it so triggering for me?" Shiloh's bottom lip quivered, seeking to prevent her cry, but she failed.

"You said it yesterday. You feel cheated too. Angry, hurt, and embarrassed. All of those are real and valid feelings to have, sweetheart," I uttered, shifting my position to face Shiloh and encouraging her to look at me.

"But maybe every trigger is not meant to break you or create fear and anxiety. Every day I am learning that God will permit some triggers because He wants to challenge you. A test to determine if you will seek Him first or wallow in the fury and pain. Maybe those triggers are presented to heal you, babygirl."

"Do you still love daddy?" Shiloh blurted, but her tone was a soft whisper.

I wavered, deliberating on the past twenty years with Quentin, and the good outweighed the bad. When we were good, it was so good. But when things got bad, they were defective beyond repair. No recall or reclamation. Our season was then, and now it's over.

"Daddy gave me you, so I will always love him and be grateful for that," I admitted. My soft sobs were now controlling the moment too.

Shiloh snuggled under my arm as we consoled each other.

"Will you ever forgive him?" she croaked.

I did not falter on this response because I'd paid Dr. Ray a lot of money to dissect forgiveness.

"Yes, Shiloh, I will. I have, but I will never forget," I stated firmly.

"How? Why?" She snickered mockingly.

"I didn't forgive daddy for his benefit, Shi. My forgiveness wasn't for Quentin at all. I forgave him for me. To save me, babygirl," I definitively declared.

Shi's countenance momentarily returned to its impassive state while she rested her head in my lap. Massaging my fingers through her scalp, we settled quietly for so long that I thought she had drifted to sleep, so her next question shocked me.

"What am I supposed to do about his baby... my... sister?

Quinn," Shiloh mumbled. Her voice was so low I barely registered what she said.

Shit! Dr. Ray didn't tell me how to respond to this. I thought, buying myself time to ponder my reply.

"Sweetie, I can't tell you how to feel about Quinn or your dad. The only thing that I can say is she *is* your sister. Your daddy's blood fuels the both of you. Think about all of the ways that you are like your father that makes you the strong, free-spirited, confident, and self-assured young lady you are," I bent to kiss her cheek, thankful to see a glimpse of a smile.

"Whatever you decide, just remember... This situation is not your fault and it's not her fault. You cannot carry the burden of your father's blunders. And neither should Quinn. But take your time. Heal, Shi. Whatever you decide, I will always support you. Ok?"

Shiloh lifted from my lap, nodding and wiping away tears. She pulled me into a firm, necessary hug. That hug comforted and restored me in ways I did not realize I needed.

"I love you, mommy."

"I love you, my sweet girl."

9

ZEKE & JULES

Zeke

I rounded the track, completing my fifth mile with Jay-Z's "Blueprint" album blasting through my ear pods. I'd been on this track almost every day since I arrived in Brooklyn three weeks ago. It was mid-July and hot as hell, but the weather was no match for my mood. I'd been unbearable and a fucking inferno, ready to combust at any moment.

I hadn't heard Jemma's voice since that night on her living room floor. It was like we were back to square one when she was somebody's wife. The extent of our communication was a random *I love you* text, an excerpt from a Nikki Giovanni poem, or a link to an old-school love song.

When I left her house that night, my Jules was supposed to go with me. We'd planned a vacation with Ezra, my cousin Myron, and Jemma's girls. Well, Ez and Myron's ladies because they'd been hot and heavy with Quaron and Maxine. By now, I should still be on a high from the two-week East Coast excursion we had planned. The first stop was a spa hideaway in the mountains, then August Wilson's *The Piano Lesson on Broadway*, and finally, travel to Washington D.C. to do all of the touristy shit that people do in chocolate city. All of those plans were canceled because of this fucking break.

Hearing those words fall out of Jemma's mouth felt like bullets riddling my body. I was prepared for the physical separation for parts of the summer because the anticipation and certainty of her face would comfort me. But the lack of communication and the unknown time frame was crippling me. Running on the track was the only time I didn't hear her sweet voice echoing in my psyche.

I finished my last lap as the exhaustion began to kick in. Sweat trickled from my body as I hunched over with my hands resting on my knees to catch my breath. The beeping sound in my ear indicated an incoming call.

"Yeah," I answered the phone.

"Yo, Lil," Ezra barked. "I'm walking towards you man."

I looked up to see my brother walking from the parking lot near the track. Shaking my head, I already knew that he was about to curse me out.

With his hands held high in frustration, Ezra yelled, "Nigga," without caring who was listening.

"Yo, Big, I'm sorry, man. I completely forgot about the basketball game."

I was supposed to meet my brother for a three-on-three game with a few of his boys from work. My mind had been so inundated with trepidation I'd missed a few scheduled events with family and friends. I hated to admit the shit, but I was fucking depressed. I missed that goddam woman like crazy.

I squeezed the bottle to shoot water in my mouth while Ezra sat on the bench I used to stretch. He knew I was struggling, and I was confident he had an opinion, but Ezra joined me in the stillness.

Several long moments depleted before I babbled, "I guess you were right, Big."

Ezra shook his head. "I don't want to be right about this, Lil. You love that woman and that woman loves you. Anybody who's around you two for five seconds can see that."

"Yeah, but you called it with her situation. She ain't a wife anymore, but she'll always be Shiloh's mother. Her entire life has revolved around her daughter. So unfortunately for me, no blessing from Shiloh, means no Zeke and Jules."

Ezra and I audibly sighed in unison.

"I'm sorry, bro. For real. You and Jemma are perfection in an imperfect and fucked up situation. But one thing I know to be true is if it's meant to be, there ain't shit that can stop it," Ezra reassured, patting me on my shoulder.

His phone rang, and mine chimed in my ear pods.

"This is Myron. I'm sure he's calling about drinks tonight," Ezra announced before answering the call.

I looked at my phone while he talked to our cousin through the speakerphone.

"What's up, cuz?" he answered jovially.

My eyes bulged, turning vacant and terrified by what I read in a text message.

"It's Aunt V. Get to the hospital right the fuck now," Myron shouted. Urgency and alarm amplified the tremble in his voice.

Jules

"Mother Holiday. Hi. Is everything OK?" I was alarmed, wondering why Mrs. Holiday would be calling me.

I visited my parents in St. Louis since the university was

officially operating on summer hours. To get my brain off of Ezekiel, I started taking a yoga class in the park. Mrs. Holiday's name on my phone screen surprised me because I'd just seen her at my mother's brunch on Sunday. I knew that Shiloh was going to stay the night with her grandparents, so I was a little concerned when I answered.

"Hi, Jemma. Well, yes and no. Shiloh is a little upset. I guess someone from the team told her about Quinton's decision."

Shit! I mutedly gritted my teeth to prevent cursing while talking to my former mother-in-law.

"Quinton just pulled up but I thought it would be best for you both to be here," she said, and I sensed her concern.

"Yes, ma'am. Thank you. I'm on my way."

I saw that Quinton called me twice while I was in yoga class, and now I know why. Pulling into the driveway of the Holiday estate, Mr. Holiday was working in the yard. I chuckled a little because this activity was his way of escaping any drama in his home. If I knew my Shiloh, she was being extra dramatic right now.

"Pop Holiday, isn't it a little too hot for you to be out here?" I asked, leaning down to kiss him on his cheek.

"It's cooler out here than it is in there," he chuckled. "Babygirl Shi is on a rampage."

"I heard. Let me go see if I can control this situation," I offered, walking towards the front door. "Don't stay out here too long, Pop."

"Send me a smoke signal or something once it's clear," he jested.

We chuckled, and I nodded.

I walked into the house and looked around for everybody, but I did not have to wait long. A glowering Shiloh shot down the steps with an expression of doom. Quinton lagged behind, appearing wholly defeated. I shot a glance over to him and lifted my brow, an unspoken signal we used through the years to determine if her behavior was due to only-child syndrome or a catastrophic event. He slightly shook his head and rubbed both hands down his face. *Catastrophic.* Honestly, it was probably a little bit of both.

"Mommy, you knew about this?" she asked in an octave a bit too high for my liking.

"First of all, hello Shiloh. Second, lower your voice. Now, calm down and ask me the question again." My tenor was gentle yet stern.

She closed her eyes and released a frustrated breath, but she calmed her little ass down.

"I'm sorry. Hi, mommy. Did you know that daddy was leaving Monroe?" Shi inquired through a quiver in her voice.

"Daddy made me aware of his decision a few days ago and we were going to tell you during the appointment with Dr. Ray," I answered truthfully.

"Oh my God. This is insane. Everything is falling apart," she stomped towards the living room like a toddler.

Shiloh was having a damn tantrum.

"Shi, sweetheart, where is this coming from? Your dad has been talking about starting his own business for a few years. Why is this such a surprise?" I asked, truly shocked at this response.

"Yeah, I know. But now... When everything is already so fuc-"

"I swear to God, Shiloh Gianna Holiday, you will lose those lips today if you continue to be disrespectful," Quinton barked in his authoritarian fatherly tone. "I know you are upset, but you gone watch ya mouth."

In an effort to minimize the frantic energy in the room, I whispered, "Why don't we all just take a breath and let's sit down to discuss this?"

This scene looked grimly familiar to our last in-office session with Dr. Ray. Our previous few joint sessions were virtual, and Shiloh was doing much better. She was taking a summer class at the satellite campus in St. Louis and coaching track at a kid's summer camp.

A few days ago, I spoke with the therapist about Quinton's decision, and he recommended that we inform Shiloh during a session. Unfortunately, the news of her dad's potential departure from the university was spreading through the track team.

For many years, Quinton had considered starting his own athletic training business, and he had several offers from professional and college football teams to be a speed coach for players. While he always entertained the idea, he never pulled the trigger until now.

"Shi, this is an opportunity that I cannot refuse. I'll be living in St. Louis so I won't be far, babygirl. We can still train if you decide to rejoin the team and have our monthly dinners. Nothing changes, sweetie pie," Quinton said. His pleading heightened his usual bass-filled tone.

Shiloh expelled a languid breath and mumbled, "Everything is changing."

I nodded.

"Yeah, it is. And change is hard, but it doesn't always have to be bad or debilitating. It's a process. And we are going to work through the steps with you, Shi," I encouraged her.

"Team Holiday may look a little different these days, but me and mommy will always be a united front for you, Shiloh. Nothing will ever change that," he uttered, looking at me for reassurance.

I gestured my agreement with a closed-mouth smile.

"We love you. You're still our ladybug," I teased, causing her to crack a slight smile.

Quinton and I jointly embraced our earthly heartbeat as a team, as parents.

"Jem, can I talk to Shiloh alone for a second?" Quinton asked.

I nodded, stepping into the connecting dining room where I found Mr. and Mrs. Holiday. Tears were streaming down Mother Holiday's beautiful face that mirrored so many features of my Shi.

I locked eyes with her before she whispered, "I'm so proud of you."

I smiled, crossing the room to join my forever in-laws. Pop Holiday put a finger to his mouth to hush us so we could adequately eavesdrop. Quinton was right, team Holiday had drastically altered, but the love between our families was eternal.

"Shi, I should've said this to you already but, babygirl, I am so sorry. I take full responsibility. This is all on me... Not your mom. I was wrong, inappropriate, and irresponsible, and I'm sorry. I will spend the rest of my days atoning for what I've done. There will never be enough words to apologize to your mom, and that's on me. But as much as it pains me -" Quinton cleared his throat. "Your mom deserves to live. To be happy, Shi. Even if it's not with me. OK?"

I temporarily lost the blood flow to my heart and oxygen to my lungs. It had been an extremely long time since I heard Quinton be this vulnerable and truthful. Shit, take responsibility for his actions. In a word, I was... bewildered.

Hearing Shiloh whimper, "I love you so much, daddy," settled my spirit.

I was far from naive, so I knew rough days were still ahead, but at least the healing could begin... For everybody.

At Shiloh's request, I stayed for an early dinner. I probably would've hung around anyway because Mrs. Holiday cooked her amazing chicken lasagna. The evening had cringeworthy moments, but we were all committed to weathering this storm.

Quinton walked me to my car and opened the passenger door. I was about to slide into the seat and close the door, but he grabbed me, preventing my departure. Gawking at him, I furrowed, then lifted my brow to encourage him to speak. He was just standing there with one hand on my door and the other stuffed in his pocket.

Those light green eyes had darkened to glassy emeralds, signaling that he was nervous. I settled in the uncomfortable stare-down while trying to decipher his silence. Internally, I hummed a tune to the rhythm of the crickets chirping as several hushed moments depleted. Quinton's free hand moved to my waist, and I immediately recoiled, but I was trapped, so I didn't have anywhere to go. He minimized the already petite space between us, and I cocked my head back to prevent him from trying to kiss me.

"Quinton," I barked defensively.

"I'm sorry, Jemma. I disrespected you in the worst and there are no excuses. Seeing Shiloh broken... I've been so fucking scared. I've lost so much already and that's my fault, but I can't lose her too, Jem," he croaked, a single tear escaping the green-eyed storm.

I shook my head, pressing a hand to the center of his chest to maintain some distance.

"You won't, Q," I promised, making eye contact with him. "You won't."

Quinton glared at me, forlorn, and finality reddened his eyes. He lifted one finger to my chest and fingered the necklace, mouthing *Jules*. He scoffed, backing away a bit more before stuffing his hands in his pockets. Aimlessly kicking around loose gravel, he stared down the street. I was ready to go and was about to announce my departure when he spoke.

"I guess if it wasn't him, it would've been somebody else," Quinton somberly said, but I wasn't sure if he was simply making a statement or asking me a question.

I pondered his words because Ezekiel was not the only man to ever show me interest. However, he was the first man to see me for simply being me. My heart believed that Ezekiel was the only somebody for me. I shrugged, observing a tiny ladybug crawling on the edge of my door seal.

I reflexively fondled my necklace and shook my head.

"No. Nobody else would do. He's sunshine in the midst of a mountain of clouds. He is the only somebody for me."

I blinked back tears as a faint smile curved my face. Quinton looked astonished by my admission. We regarded each other for several prolonged heartbeats. The blaring ring echoing in my car canceled the impending argument brewing.

I checked the screen to see that Quaron was calling me. I saw a text from her earlier but hadn't reviewed it. My phone's Bluetooth automatically connected to my car. I put a finger up to Quinton and leaned into my car to answer.

"Hey, Roni. What's up?"

"Jemma, where are you? I've been texting for the past hour," she said at an octave higher than I was accustomed to.

"I'm at your -"

She quickly cut me off.

"Ezekiel's mom. Mrs. Green is in the hospital. Jemma, it doesn't look good."

My heart crashed to my stomach. I heard Quaron's words, but the last sentence did not thoroughly register. *Zeke's mom was dying?* Ezekiel's mother had been dealing with health issues since she contracted the coronavirus, but she was improving. At least, I thought she was.

"Jemma, did you hear me?" Roni blurted.

She was so loud I was certain Quinton heard every word. I glanced up at him, still standing outside of my car. His expression confirmed that he heard because it was teetering between placid and perturbed simultaneously.

"Yeah. Um, yes. Can you check flights for me? I want to leave tonight," I instructed, hopping into my car because I had to go.

"J, where are you going?" Quinton asked, already knowing the answer.

"To *him*."

10

ZEKE & JULES

Zeke

Mama taught us to never use the word *hate,* but at this moment, I hated the hospital. Sterile white walls, bland stale odor, and rude, inattentive staff were not my idea of a good time. I leaned against the wall in the waiting room on the intensive care floor and watched as family members packed in this small space. It was pretty surreal because typically, in these situations, my mother would be the first person at the hospital visiting family and friends and the last to leave. But this time, we were here for Mama. *Praying* for Mama.

"Daddy." I heard the tear-filled voice before I saw my peanut's face.

"YaYa. Come here babygirl."

"Is granny OK? Can I see her?" My daughter Eriya asked, her face covered in tears.

"No, baby, not yet. As soon as we can, me and you, we'll go together, OK."

"Have you talked to EJ?"

"No. He's several hours ahead of us and I don't want to alarm him unless I have to. OK."

She nodded and nestled under my shoulder. My son, Ezekiel, was on a safari trip with his school. I had an emergency number, but I didn't want to disrupt his experience unless absolutely necessary. *I pray that it's not necessary.*

After comforting YaYa with a kiss atop her head, I looked up to see my ex-wife, Michelle, walking into the waiting room. The years had been good to her. She'd picked up a bit of weight but carried it well because of her height. Long hair the color of coal was now cut into a sleek old-school Toni Braxton cut. Big almond eyes matched full pouty lips, lending to her exotic appearance. The years since our divorce have also helped us be... Not friends, but friendly.

"Zeke, hey. How's mom?" She asked, pulling me into a hug.

"We don't know much yet. They believe she had a heart attack but there was also something with her lungs so..." I shrugged as my voice faded. "We don't know."

"Oh my God," she gasped, placing a hand over her mouth as her eyes flooded with tears.

"Come here." I pulled her into my arms alongside my daughter.

I lifted my head in response to Ezra calling my name. A woman with skin the color of clay dressed in a white coat stood in the doorway, waiting for the family to gather. I concentrated on her eyes to determine if they held sympathy or hope. She wore an expressionless poker face but greeted us with a faint smile when me and Myron approached. The doctor signaled her head for us to step into the hallway.

"Hello, I am Dr. Abena Lincoln, one of the cardiologists on

staff. We have a host of specialists caring for Mrs. Green, but right now, her heart is our greatest concern."

We nodded in unison, desperate for her to deliver some positive news.

"I believe Mrs. Green has suffered a pulmonary edema which in layman's terms is fluid surrounding the heart and lungs. We have her in a medically-induced coma to allow her body to rest. Several medications are helping drain as much of the fluid as possible. She is stable but in a very serious condition. The next few days are critical, but we are doing absolutely everything we can."

She nodded, then smiled. Ezra walked away, clutching his nape.

"When can we see her?" I asked.

"The nurse will notify you soon. But, please, only two family members in the room at a time."

Dr. Lincoln strolled away. I watched her disappear down the hallway as if it was all a dream. I wanted to move, but my feet felt like blocks of cement. Peering around, I witnessed Mama's three boys fall into our usual dispositions during times of crisis. Ezra was in fight or flight mode, whereas Myron was stoic, basically numb to reality. As for me, I was a thinker, forecasting and calculating all of the possibilities.

Hours later, I rubbed my dry eyes, endeavoring to erase the vision of my petite and feisty mother lying in a hospital bed with tubes sprouting from everywhere. She looked like she was in a restful slumber until the machines pumped air through her body, causing her chest to expand and shrink.

We'd been at the hospital for over twelve hours. The last time I peeked at my watch was after six in the morning. Thankfully, the waiting room was not as crowded anymore. I glanced around to see my brother still staring out of the window. He probably hadn't slept at all. While we were both close to our mother, she and Ezra had a special relationship, especially since he was the son who stayed in Brooklyn. If something happened to Mama, the devastation would be real for all of us, but for Ez, it would be a catastrophic blow to his well-being.

I caressed Eriya's soft curls as she slept in my lap. Michelle lightly snored as she rested on my shoulder. Releasing an exasperated breath, I blinked, trying for moisture in my eyes one more time.

"Zeke," Myron whispered.

"Hmm," I responded but never opened my eyes.

"Maybe you should get them home. Everybody needs to get some rest."

I nodded. "I will. Just give a minute. I will."

At this point, I believe I was slightly delirious and in disbelief. Hearing the doctor tell us that my mother was in a coma and we'd just have to wait for her to hopefully wake up. *Hopefully. What the fuck did she mean, hopefully?* Vesta Green was the strongest person I knew. She had to wake up. Dammit, she was going to wake up. *God, please let her wake up.*

"Lil, I'm going to get coffee," Ezra announced.

"I'm good."

I heard my phone chime, but I didn't have the energy to look at it. Everyone I needed to answer to was in this room except for my son, and I was certain it wasn't EJ.

"Lil," Ezra said again, tapping me on my shoulder.

"What, bro? Damn," I shouted, swatting his hand away from me.

He motioned his head to the door. I fingered my eyes once again because I had to be dreaming. Jemma had inundated my fantasies since I reluctantly walked away from her weeks ago. But was my Jules standing before me looking absolutely stunning? Her fresh face was bare, and her braids were pulled into a bun. She was casually dressed in a flowy maxi dress, a denim jacket, and Gucci slides. Still, she was the most mesmerizing thing I'd ever seen.

'*Jules*,' I muttered in a mere whisper. Her pretty brown eyes landed on me, then dropped to Eriya and back up to Michelle. *Shit! Michelle.* She nibbled the inside of her cheek and nervously twiddled her fingers.

I never disjointed my eyes from her when I tapped both YaYa and Michelle, encouraging them to lift up. My brain was telling me to run to her, but my feet had a mind of their own. Slowly ambling, I eliminated the break between us. *Break.* It was what she requested, but she was here, so *fuck a break*! I needed my lady.

I frantically cupped the curves of her face, and she returned the sentiment.

"Zee," she whispered, gazing directly into my stinging eyes.

I collapsed into her arms and finally released the distress, panic, and tears I'd been holding for hours. Uncontrollably wailing, I buried my dampened face into her floral-scented neck. The vigor of my bawling caused me to push our bodies into the hallway. I pressed her against the wall, still concealing my face.

"Baby, I'm here. I got you, Zeke," Jemma whispered, kissing and wiping my tears away.

"How are you here?" I mumbled, still seeking respite in the scented folds of her flesh.

"Quaron called me last night. I got the first flight out. I didn't mean to just show up. But I needed to see you. I needed to be here for you. I tried to call but it went straight to voicemail. I dropped my location, but-" She was rambling.

I vigorously shook my head to cease her rant because I did not require any explanation.

"Jules, baby, stop. I'm so fucking happy you're here right now. I needed you."

"How is Mrs. Green?"

"In a coma. The next few days are critical."

"Ezekiel," she whimpered, coupling our foreheads. "I'm so sorry."

I closed my eyes. "Can you stay? Please tell me you can stay."

I felt her head bob up and down against my skin.

"Use your words, wordsmith," I teased.

"For as long as you need me, babe."

We exchanged inhales and exhales as I drew her body into mine tighter. Her warm flesh, her aroma, mellowed me... she healed me.

"I missed you," I confessed, swiping a loose braid from her eyes because I'd destroyed the bun.

"I love you." The sound of Jemma's confession was like music to my ears.

Jules

For a brief second, my heart fell to my ass when I saw Ezekiel in the waiting room. Exhaustion and defeat were written all over his scowl. But he was being comforted... By another woman.

I didn't want to be *that* type of chick, but my past demons caused me to pause and second-guess my decision to come. Especially when my eyes landed on a beautiful woman with skin the color of almond milk and a curvier physique than mine lying on Ezekiel's shoulder.

Eriya's cute face was familiar to me, but this woman... Her presence, shit, her coziness with him made me nauseous. *Michelle.*

I'd never seen a photo, but I knew this was his ex-wife. Once she lifted and her sable eyes connected with mine, Zeke's children resided there.

But my selfish and self-conscious thoughts dissipated when his stately, dejected body trampled over to me with urgency in every step. My only focus was providing solace for him.

After the passionate, emotional caress that I wish we could've lingered in for eternity concluded, Ezekiel clutched my hand, escorting me into the waiting room. Eriya's eyes widened as her apparent suspicions were confirmed. Like everyone else, we had not disclosed our relationship to our daughters. EJ was well aware, but apparently, so were Shiloh and Eriya, given my daughter's admittance during the therapy session and the expression on his daughter's face.

"Dr. Holiday," Eriya said with a questioning tone.

"Hello, Eriya. I'm so sorry to hear about your grandmother," I returned, swiping a comforting hand down her arm.

I glanced over to the woman, intently observing the exchange. She greeted me with a wry smile, and I returned the sentiment.

"Michelle, I want you to meet my girlfriend, Dr. Jemma Holiday," Zeke announced.

For whatever reason, I expected him to stammer through the introduction, but he was his usual calm, confident, and sexy self.

"It's nice to meet you, Michelle," I uttered, mirroring his confident tenor.

"Nice to meet you as well, Dr. Holiday."

"Please, call me Jemma."

She nodded.

"Zeke, we're going to head out. Call me once mom can have visitors," Michelle relayed before leaning in to kiss him on the cheek.

"Thank you for coming," he murmured before turning to his daughter.

"Come here, babygirl," Zeke commanded, kissing into a bushel of curls. "Granny is going to be fine, OK? I promise I'll call as soon as I hear something."

Eriya nodded. "You should get some rest too, daddy."

"I will. I'm going to chat with the doctor and then head home."

"I love you," Eriya whimpered.

"I love you more," Ezekiel declared.

A couple hours later, Ezekiel and I climbed the steps of his brownstone. Our sluggish amble signified exhaustion. Zeke hit a few numbers on the keypad to unlock the door.

"Shit," he whispered.

"What's wrong?" I asked, resting my hand on the small of his back.

He stepped aside, revealing cans of paint, flooring samples, and other materials lined up against the foyer wall.

"I'm in the middle of renovations to sell this place. If I'd known you were coming, I would've-"

I placed two fingers on his lips to silence him.

"Zeke, it's fine. There's a bed and a bathroom, right?" I teased.

He chuckled, and seeing a smile on his face felt so good, even if it was temporary.

"We have all of the basics."

I advanced further into the house, and he was not lying. Only the essentials were accessible. The kitchen cabinets were stripped and draped with a protective covering. The only operable appliance was the refrigerator. I laughed because while the living room only had a reclining chair and a table, a massive, seventy-plus-inch television sat on a stand. *The basics.*

We picked up bagel sandwiches and coffee from a shop not far from his house. I sat on the one bar stool while he leaned against the counter. We ate in silence. Fatigue was only partially responsible for the dismayed guise; worry was imprinted on his glorious face.

"She can't die," he blurted.

My eyes shot up to peer at him. Those chocolate irises were reddened and weary. Tears streamed down his cheeks, but his profile remained stoic.

"Babe, she won't. She's strong. From what I've heard from you, your mom's a fighter."

He nodded.

"What can I do?" I muttered, moving closer to wrap my arms around his waist.

Swiping away his tears with my thumb, I repeated my question.

"Zee, what can I do?"

His breathing was erratic as he cried, "Take the pain away, Jules. Please, baby."

His salty tears commingled with mine as I bound my forehead to his. The soft, delicate kisses were like whispers to every pained crease on his face. Our tongues collided, and we both expelled a sigh of relief. It had been too long since I had experienced my favorite lover. I missed this man more than words could express.

Ezekiel grabbed fists full of my braids, deepening the kiss. Our tongues played tug-of-war as they fought to achieve a delicious sensation. A firm, thick rod pressed into my stomach. Even after months of sex with this man, his dick still took my breath away.

My center was drenched and throbbing with a need only he could satisfy. I practically ripped the t-shirt from his flesh, desperate to be cloaked by his skin. The way we panted with urgency, I didn't see the need to bother with foreplay. Ezekiel released his strength from his sweatpants, and my mouth watered. I was in a welcomed conundrum. Did I want him in my mouth or my pussy?

Ezekiel solved my unmentioned dilemma. He lifted my dress and turned my body around in one swift motion. My kitty ached, and my breasts were sore from lusting for this man for weeks. Although Zeke asked me to take his pain away, I surrendered to his need for control.

Fire shot through my core when Zeke entered me from behind. The backward motion of my ass met the forward thrust of his dick, creating the perfect tempo. He pounded into me with relentless perseverance. Our grunts and groans harmonized in echoing melodies.

"Zee, I'm not going to make it," I breathed in long, surrendering moans.

"Shit, shit. Me either, baby. Shit," he winced, unable to disguise his impending climax.

Our lovemaking sessions usually lasted for hours. Ezekiel was an expert at prolonging my orgasm. But tonight, we almost combusted after the first touch. He grabbed my hands, shackling my wrists with one hand while his other hand firmly clutched my hips. Zeke routed every single inch of his thickness into me. Over and over and over again, he knocked against my wet walls.

Zeal surged through my veins, and passion seeped through my pores like an inferno. I was coming... and hard. His grip grew tighter, and pounding intensified as ripples of ecstasy throbbed, causing an unexplained explosion.

"Zeke!" I shouted,

"Jules, fuck!" he bellowed.

My cheek was pressed to the cold granite while Ezekiel rested against my back. The rhythm of his heart's thudder was rocking me to sleep. He unhurriedly lifted me, guiding my body up with him. Nestling in the folds of my neck, I shivered from his caress. His erection was still present inside of me. As that thing steadily shrunk, the tingling sensation between my legs as that thing steadily shrunk made me quiver.

Zeke repositioned me to face him. This man was beautiful, but he was beautifully broken at this moment. The chiseled carving of his cheeks appeared muted by sadness. But even in his misery, this man was riveting. A magnetism so potent he had me under a spell. He glared at me; his expression was serious, reflective.

"Thank you for showing up for me," he expressed, baritone low and raspy.

"Every fucking time, babe."

11

ZEKE

I was enjoying my second favorite pastime... Watching Jemma sleep. When we arrived at my place yesterday, I couldn't resist devouring her sweet essence. I needed something to help me escape reality, and my Jules was the best place to seek refuge. Even if it was only temporary.

Jemma sat with me in the hospital for most of the day. She periodically nodded on my shoulder as we watched my mother. It took hours for me to convince her to let me take her home so she could get some rest. During the drive home, we decided to pick up food at a neighborhood Jamaican restaurant for an early dinner.

We assumed the same position as the day before, with her perched at the island and me leaning against the countertop, eating in silence. Jemma used her sorcery once again to persuade me to get some sleep. The way she slid down on my firmness had me momentarily knocked out, but extended slumber evaded me. My talk with the doctor earlier had me uneasy and scared as fuck. *The next few days are critical. You should consider making some decisions just in case things take a turn.*

My mother was still in a medically-induced coma. Her vitals were not consistently remaining stabilized, so the doctors were concerned about lung function percentage. My keen ability to restore damaged situations would not work for this. I was a fixer, but I felt utterly helpless. There was no strategic plan or business forecast that I could leverage to rectify my mother's condition. All I knew to do was what Vesta Green taught me... Pray. Since the day I received the call about Mama, I've begged God to spare her life.

When Jemma fell asleep, I grabbed my keys and headed right back to the hospital. For some reason, I knew that Ezra and Myron would be there. We just sat around Mama's bedside like three pitiful little orphaned boys. Our rock, our foundation, was crumbling right before our eyes, and we were weak.

I meandered into my house a little after ten o'clock at night. Expecting Jemma to be awake by now, I carried the box of warm cookies I had bought into the bedroom, but Jemma was still asleep. Settling the box on the nightstand, I leaned against the mattress, stroking a finger down her nose. She roused a little but didn't immediately awaken. I circled my thumb at the ball of her cheeks, an action I knew was guaranteed to make her smile.

"Are you counting freckles again?" Jemma asked, stretching to extend her half-naked body.

A black thin-strapped tank top and a matching thong barely concealed her bulbous titties. And that ass... damn. That ass swallowed the cotton material. I'd only been in the room for five minutes, and my dick was already hard.

"You always mess up my count," I teased.

Jemma shifted in the bed to make room for me. She patted the mattress, encouraging me to join her. I stepped out of my shorts and removed my t-shirt before climbing into bed. My back pressed into her chest as she draped her legs across my body. I chuckled because Jules' legs were petite and thick compared to my long limbs. She rested her chin atop my bald head and absently rubbed her fingertips up and down my arm, tracing the outline of my tattoos.

"Did you sleep OK?" I asked, mimicking her motions up and down her thigh.

"Yes. I woke up looking for you but then I saw your text."

"Why didn't you call me?" I continued to probe, gliding her hand up to my mouth for a peck.

"I figured you needed some space. I talked to Shiloh for a little while then went back to sleep."

"How is she?"

I was a little reluctant to inquire since Jemma, and I hadn't discussed our conversation from the last time we saw each other. Since she arrived two days ago, I'd wondered what had transpired over the past several weeks since our *break.*

"She's better. We are just taking things one day at a time," she sighed, kissing my cheek. "We can talk about that another time. How's your mom?"

"The same. No change," I answered, shifting my stance to face her. "Jules, I actually want to talk about it now."

"Talk about what?" She creased her forehead. I could tell she did not want to broach this subject.

"Me. You. Shiloh. The way we left things..." My voice faded.

Jemma fidgeted with her necklace, which I learned was a clear sign that she was either anxious and/or thinking. In a short amount of time, I learned the intricacies of Jemma Jule Holiday. She lacked a poker face, so when direct eye contact was avoided, Jules had something to say but did not want to express herself. My time with her also taught me to give her space to reflect. I would remain mute for as long as she needed me to.

"Shiloh is still devastated. Some days she doesn't want to get out of the bed but like I said, we... She is taking it one day at a time." Jemma spoke but wouldn't look at me. A nervous shrug now accompanied her fiddling.

"Where does she think you are right now?" I queried.

"New York," she whispered.

"With me?"

She nodded.

"And how did that conversation go?"

Jemma pursed her lips, shaking her head, but she remained wordless. I lifted her chin and then softly kissed her, allowing my mouth to linger over her lips.

"Use your words," I breathily uttered, inspiring her with another peck.

"I just left. When Roni called to tell me about your mother, all I could do was figure out how to get to you as quickly as possible," she bashfully murmured.

I recalled the exact second when Jemma appeared at the hospital carrying only a weekender bag. My Jules didn't pack light to go anywhere, so it was clear to me that she departed in haste.

"Baby," I whimpered, my words refusing to form correctly.

I had been on an emotional roller coaster for the last three days, and Jemma's actions just took me over the top. My Jules walked away, not knowing what awaited her back home with Shiloh or even her ex. She reciprocated, showing up for me like I'd done for her, and that shit touched a nigga behind his chest.

"You know when I told you that I love you more than you know?" I asked, not caring about the tears streaming down my face.

Jemma nodded, her misty eyes copying mine. We were still nestled in a bit of a cocoon. We were like leeches, my every inhale attached to her exhale, guzzling every bit of air she would allow. Our bodies were endlessly entangled, unable to decipher my skin from hers.

"Jemma, I carry you with me like the sun, the moon, and the stars. You are *everywhere*. After my divorce, I never wanted to be in that type of relationship again. Sure, I wanted friends, companionship, intimacy, but not the commitment. But the moment you turned around to greet me in that restaurant wearing the hell out of that purple dress, I saw *forever* with you, Jemma. And it fucked me up because I believed that I would have to watch you from the sideline," I poured out my heart, deeply inhaling to get my shit together. "I took the provost job because I knew that I deserved it, but more importantly, I needed to be *close* to you. To *fucking breath your air*, baby. To show you *your worth* even if I didn't reap the benefits."

"Zee," she cried, eyes wide in disbelief.

"So when I say I love you more than you will ever know, that's why. I sacrificed everything just to be near you. Win or lose."

Jemma adjusted to straddle me. Her tears drizzled down my chest as we gazed at each other. Even with my declaration, fear and fascination occupied her beautiful chestnut eyes. I reached up to loosen her ponytail, massaging my fingers through her scalp before drawing her face to mine. Licking against the seam of her lips, I claimed her mouth with a demanding mastery. Jemma's saccharine kisses were new to me every damn time. I loved the way she sucked my tongue with the same passion that she engulfed my dick.

I squeezed and kneaded her ass, causing her hot, moist kitty to sway against my distended member. My Jules melodically moaned, creating a soundtrack just for us.

My shit was ready to erupt when she swiped her tongue down my neck, trailing a path to my chest. Voluptuous hips swaying against my erection, serene whimpers of pleasure, and her mouth on my nipples had me fucking feeble. But I found enough strength to partake in my number one favorite pastime, tasting my Jules.

"Come here, Jemma," I commanded, and she knew exactly what I meant.

I wanted that sweet ass pussy on my face.

"Zee, baby, I'm almost there."

"Come. Now," I muttered, my voice was even more demanding.

Jemma shimmied up the length of my body like she was climbing a tree. To my delight, her thong was drenched.

"Mmm. This is what I've been missing. My beard has been dry without you, baby. I need your moisture, Jules. All of it."

I slid her thong to the side and licked her plump folds in elongated swipes, wasting no time diving in. Usually, I prayed over my meal, but I was too famished. Forgiveness would be requested later.

My tongue frolicked and pranced in her pussy to the rhythm of her moans. Jemma's hands were draped across the top of the tufted headboard while her forehead settled against the plush fabric. I clutched her ass, but my Jules required no guidance. She rode my face at a determined tempo. I licked, lapped, suckled, and tongue-kissed her juicy essence until she sheened my beard with her dewy wonder.

I firmly pressed my hands to the lower part of her thighs to lift her body from my face. I held her lethargic frame in the air until I was able to slide down the bed a bit. Jemma completely collapsed against the headboard, moaning through the aftershocks.

She was still on her knees, so I positioned myself behind her, wrapping my arms around her waist. Snuggling into her body, I peppered a series of *Jules*-flavored kisses down the side of her neck.

Journeying my shaft up and down the slit of her ass, I whispered, "I love you."

"I love you, Zeke," she practically groaned.

Jemma reached one hand up to caress my neck before I entered her slowly. My manhood wanted to proceed at an accelerated pace, but I desired to mosey around in her depths. Demonstrate my love with more than just words.

She gasped, uttering, "Mmm, baby."

I whispered, "No more breaks, Jules. Promise me," I urged, pumping into her.

I didn't realize I was crying again until my voice croaked.

"Promise me, Jules," I wept through dallying yet determined strokes.

"No breaks, baby. I promise," she bayed, leaning her head to the side to kiss me. "Ask me again, Zee. Ask me what my heart needs."

"Jules," I growled, the orgasm simmering like hot fire. "What do you need, babe?"

"*You*, Ezekiel. My heart needs **you**!" she shouted that last word through a forceful orgasm.

I was right behind her, growling out my gratification. "Jemma, shit."

We repositioned so she could lay her naked flesh against my frame. All it took was about five seconds, and she was snoring lightly. I glared at the ceiling fan, reminiscing on what we just experienced. After the passion and adoration verbally and physically expressed through our lovemaking, I was confident *she* was the only way I wanted to spend my forever.

12

ZEKE & JULES

Jules

The August heat was sweltering as I trekked from the administration building to my car after a long day. The campus was still a ghost town, but the peace and quiet would not last much longer. The new school year was starting in a couple weeks, and I was drowning in deadlines. When my phone chimed, I waved at the grounds workers and maintenance staff, preparing for the influx of students.

The Good Doctor: I miss you.

The wave of happiness was only momentary because I missed him too. Although I lived in Monroe City most of my adult life, it felt different without Ezekiel's presence. I wanted to stay in New York to support him, but I had to return home back to my regular schedule.

Me: I miss you.

I responded to his text just as I passed the reception desk. Sharon was intently focused on a phone call when I tossed up a hand to greet her. I chuckled because Sharon claimed she was retiring every year, and every August, when I returned from summer vacation, she was right in the same position. Her index finger shot up, motioning for me to pause. She ended the call and turned in the office chair to face me.

"Hey, Dr. Holiday. Welcome back."

"Ms. Sharon, what are you doing here? Didn't we give you a retirement party in May?" I chortled, rounding the desk to hug her.

I'd been hibernating in my office all day, so I did not realize Sharon was in the building.

"Girl, I know, but when I spent all day, everyday with my grandkids, I said, no, ma'am. This is not the life for me," she chuckled. "I'm just working part time. Three days a week. They will probably have to bury me in this place."

I smiled because Sharon was the heart of Monroe University and would forever be cherished. She worked at the school for forty years since she was a twenty-year-old single mother with three kids. Her circumstance didn't prevent her from finally finishing her bachelor's degree and working up the administrative ranks.

"Well, just seeing your face has made my day," I acknowledged, giving her a high five.

"Looks like somebody else is trying to make your day. This delivery is for you," Sharon smirked, lifting a curious brow. "Does Dr. Holiday have a secret admirer or is the coach trying to get that old thang back?"

I dropped my head and hollered, laughing.

"Mind your business, ma'am," I giggled, retrieving the gorgeous bouquet of red roses.

Walking to my car, I was eager to open the note. I did not have to question the sender because Zeke had been showering me with flowers and gifts since I left New York.

I stayed with him for two weeks; it was the most emotionally charged fourteen days of my life. Watching the man I loved struggle with his mother's failing health was heartbreaking. Zeke spent at least twelve hours a day by Mrs. Green's bedside with no change.

The morning I stayed at his place to have a virtual therapy session with Shiloh and Quinton, Ezekiel called me back to back twice. But once I called him back, he didn't answer. I tried his phone at least twenty times before hopping in an Uber to the hospital. Praying during the entire thirty-minute ride, I hoped Mrs. Green hadn't taken a turn for the worse.

I recalled feeling breathless and nauseous when I hurried down the hallway of the intensive care floor to see Michelle and Eriya crying. Pressing a hand over my mouth, I just knew I would vomit. I abruptly halted my amble because I needed a minute before finding Zeke. He appeared in the hallway, rubbing a hand down his face. The gap separating us felt endless as my feet scurried to get to him.

"Zee," I exclaimed in a shaky whisper.

Even with a faint murmur, he heard me. Ezekiel diminished our distance with quick long strides. I gripped the sides of his face as our eyes danced back and forth in a frenzy. He was hushed, aside from the laborious breaths he fought to exhale.

"Zee," I said again, questioningly.

"She's awake," he croaked. His heavy stately frame crashed into me when he released a clamorous sob.

I blinked back tears, recollecting that day as I opened the card attached to the flowers.

Jules, baby, I miss you so much. Thank you for everything. I don't know

how I would have survived one of the toughest times in my life. You still
don't know how much I love you. I'm counting down the weeks until I
can show you.
Love Forever, Zeke
P.S. Mama says hello, and she's waiting for her cashew brittle.

I giggled, swiping away a stray tear. Mrs. Green and I had become fast friends since God opened her eyes that Friday afternoon after seven days in a coma. When Zeke asked me to go into her room with him, I was reluctant because this was not how I wanted to meet his mother.

Ezekiel carried her beautiful chocolate skin and almond-shaped eyes. Meticulously parted, uncoiled salt and pepper curls framed her round face. She was fairly alert but whispered because of the intubation tube. Mrs. Green's coffee-colored orbs brightened at the sight of Ezekiel. I peered around the room to see Ezra seated next to her bed with his head resting in the palm of his mother's hand. Myron leaned against a wall in the corner, shaking his head with a perplexed expression.

Mrs. Vesta Green was *a miracle*. While everyone in the room was well aware, she wore a visage of confusion and uncertainty.

"She doesn't remember anything," Ezekiel whispered to me.

I nodded, keeping my distance and observing the room. Ezra stood to his full height, then bent close to her face.

"Ma, I'm going to step out for some air. I'll be right back, OK? I promise," Ezra whimpered.

I'd never heard his voice sound so small. He patted his brother on the shoulder and kissed me on the cheek before exiting the room. Ezekiel took his place at the side of their mother's bed. Her faint smile melted my heart. To my surprise, she shifted her eyes to me.

"Mama, this is my Jules," Zeke introduced, then winked at me.

Mrs. Green softly tapped two fingers on her bed. She appeared to crook one finger for me to come closer. I looked at Ezekiel, who nodded, signaling me to oblige.

"Hi, Mrs. Green. It's a pleasure to meet you."

She slowly bobbed her head. I noticed that she was attempting to speak, so I shortened the space so that I could hear her.

"My son loves you," she rasped, tenor throaty.

I could not contain the broad beam that adorned my face.

"I love your son too," I admitted, stroking my thumb across the top of her hand.

The sound of my phone ringing adjourned my reminiscing.

"I'm getting in the car," I knew it was Maxine calling me because I was late.

Tomorrow was my birthday, and Maxi and Roni were taking me to dinner.

"Bring ya ass. I'm two margaritas in. You have some catching up to do," she cackled.

"Order my shit now. I'm on my way," I demanded jokingly.

After too many lobster tacos, shrimp enchiladas, three margaritas, and five hours of amusement, I schlepped into my house almost at midnight. My buzz was minimal, but I was sleepy as hell. I kicked off my shoes and dropped my work bag in the mudroom. Crossing the threshold into my kitchen, I turned on a brighter light and abruptly halted. A mini bundt cake with a single candle and a yellow envelope set on my island. *What the fuck?*

Just as I was about to take the hell off running because somebody had to be in my house, my phone rang. I checked the screen, and I eased... but only slightly.

"Hey," I answered the video call. My eyes roamed around my house to determine if anything else was out of the ordinary.

"Light the candle so I can sing happy birthday." Zeke's baritone made my belly rumble.

"What? How did you-?"

He interrupted and repeated, "Light the candle, Jules."

"It's not my birthday yet?" I teased.

"It is in New York," he said with the sexiest smirk.

Zeke was lying in bed shirtless, and I desired for him to move the camera a few inches lower. I propped my phone against a canister and grabbed a lighter. He smiled, watching me light the candle.

"Happy birthday to you. Happy birthday, my baby Jules. Happy birthday to you," he sang, unable to contain his boisterous laugh.

I giggled, closing my eyes to blow out the candle.

"What did you wish for?" he asked.

"You."

～

"Good morning, gorgeous," I greeted, eyeing myself in the full-length mirror. "Happy birthday, Jemma Jule," I cited, being the second to celebrate my forty-first birthday.

Ezekiel was the first. We talked for hours last night while I demolished the cinnamon crunch bundt cake. I was completely drained, but the excitement of my birthday always boosted my energy.

Since red was my signature color, I often wore the shade on my birthday. Since the day was Friday and school was not officially back in session, I dressed more casually than usual. Taking a last look at my curves in the red strapless jumper, I grabbed my denim jacket and Neverful bag and hurried out of the house.

My schedule was insane today, so I decided to call Ezekiel before leaving the house, to no avail. We were up pretty late last night, but it was unlike him not to answer my calls, and when he did, I usually got a text message informing me that he would call me right back. I have yet to receive those. Pulling into my parking space on campus, I tried him one more time. *Voicemail.*

I dismissed any uneasy feelings and exited the car. I smiled at the sight of the maroon and gold balloons decorating the front of the administration building. Today was the staff barbeque, and the catering employees were setting up a feast. Before the hustle and bustle of the new year, this was a great opportunity to show appreciation for the staff working tirelessly throughout the summer to beautify the campus for another round of scholars.

It was honestly a little bittersweet for me because Ezekiel would not be here. He was still overseeing his mother's care. We'd planned for me to travel to New York this weekend, but Shiloh unexpectedly planned a weekend getaway for the two of us. While a break from Zeke would never again enter my vocabulary, he understood that I needed this time with Shiloh. I just had to be patient and see him when he returned to Monroe City in a couple weeks.

"Happy birthday, Dr. Holiday," Sharon quipped, pulling me in for a hug.

"Thank you, Sharon."

A few other colleagues greeted me and wished me a happy birthday as I navigated the hallways heading toward my office. I opened the door and practically burst into tears because every square foot of my office was covered with red roses. My desk was swamped with gift boxes of various styles. I was so giddy, I fumbled with my phone to call Zeke and once again... His ass didn't answer.

Zeke

Voicemail. I snickered, ignoring Jemma's call for the third time. I knew she was going to be pissed, but I wasn't ready for her to know that I was in town yet. The new semester was starting in a couple of weeks, and I told the university I would not return until then, but I had to be here for my lady. Jules' birthday was today, and I couldn't miss the opportunity to surprise her. I sneaked into her house last night to deliver the card and cake, so it was waiting for her when she got home.

The administrative staff was having their annual back-to-school barbeque today on the quad and using that time to celebrate Jemma's birthday. I debated showing up there, but I knew she was still apprehensive about making our relationship public. Maxine and Quaron got Jemma out of the house last night, and they were helping me plan a surprise dinner tonight, so I would have to wait several more hours before I could kiss her. They'd even let Shiloh in on the secret, and surprisingly, she was a vital part of the plan, pretending to occupy her mom's schedule this weekend.

I was counting on the building being empty since staff appreciation activities were going on throughout the campus. Aside from my daughter, Maxi, Quaron, Shiloh, and my assistant were the only other people who knew I was back in Monroe City.

"Good morning, Dr. Green. Welcome back."

"Thank you, Pamela."

"How is your mother?"

"Much better. She's giving them hell at the rehab center," I chuckled.

My mother was a living, breathing miracle. She sustained minor disabilities, given the severity of her condition. Mama would spend the next few weeks in occupational therapy to strengthen her coordination and balance. But other than that, the doctors expected her to recover fully.

"You have an urgent meeting request that came in this morning. I added it to your task list," Pamela said, and I nodded.

I entered my office for the first time in several weeks. The wooden fixtures were shining, and the lemon aroma wafted in the air indicating that the office was recently cleaned. I was ecstatic to be back because that meant that my life was not turned upside down by my mother's health or unfortunate demise. I shook my head, dismissing that thought from my psyche.

Jemma's beautiful face popped up on the screen again. I declined the call again, opting to send her a text message so that she wouldn't worry or, worse, call my mother. Jules and Mama immediately connected, which was no surprise to me. Many of my mother's qualities lived in Jemma as well. As my mother slowly regained her strength, Jules decorated her room with fresh flowers daily. She massaged her achy hands and painted her nails. They laughed and talked as if I wasn't in the room. Their bond had continued to grow over time, including phone conversations a few times a week. So Jemma calling my mother to determine my whereabouts would not be abnormal.

Me: Hey, baby. I'm at a therapy session with Mama. Can I call you later?

Jules: Hey, babe. I was just about to call my friend. Tell her to behave with the therapist.

Me: You're asking for a lot, love. LOL

Jules: Wishful thinking. LOL.

Jules: Zee... the roses... the gifts. Thank you.

Jemma attached a picture of her office; everything was arranged to my specifications.

Me: You're welcome. I love you.

Jules: I love you more than you know.

. . .

I logged into my computer, smiling at Jemma's sentiment and thankful that I'd averted a potential disaster. The task that my assistant mentioned popped onto the screen, and I was temporarily frozen after seeing the requestor's name. I glanced at my watch to see the time. The requested meeting time was in ten minutes. I grabbed my shades and headed out of the office, instructing Pamela to text me if there was an emergency.

I carefully navigated across campus to ensure I didn't accidentally run into Jemma or anyone from my office. Deciding to drive, I bypassed one of many parking spaces reserved for me across campus and parked in an empty space. My heavy feet wandered down the halls, eyeing the historical plaques and awards before I walked through the corridor.

Monroe University was one of the most beautiful campuses I'd ever seen. I stood silently admiring the meticulously manicured grass trimmed in the shape of the school's crest. A small group of students were camped on the grassy area, unaware of my presence.

"Dr. Green."

A voice thundered from behind me. I turned around to view the perpetrator.

"Coach Holiday," I greeted. A querying smirk streaked my face.

"We need to talk," Quinton said with his arms crossed as our leers dueled.

I snickered, spinning back around to face the track. Coach Holiday stepped beside me. His focus was straight ahead, mirroring mine.

"Jemma and I had our first date right in the middle of this field. She was the prettiest girl I'd ever laid my eyes on. Jemma was perfect. I hung on her every word. I'm sure you can relate."

I remained wordless, but I nodded because I absolutely could relate. Jules had me spellbound at hello.

"When she got pregnant I was fucked up about it. I came to this track and ran until my legs were like Jello. We were too young, too naïve, and had too much life to live. But when Jem looked at me with a sparkle of fear and hope in her eyes, I needed our baby to bind us forever. I took that shit for granted," Quinton disclosed, holding a deep inhale before he slowly exhaled.

"I diminished that sparkle. Her light no longer belongs to me. I see her glimmer again when she looks at you and it fucks me up everytime."

I scoffed, rubbing a hand down my beard.

"Did you know that the moon actually spends almost as much time in the sky during the day that it does at night?" I asked, my focus shifting up to the clouds.

"Nah, I can't say that I've ever thought about it."

I bobbed my head, sliding my sunglasses up my face. I squinted, peering at Quinton for the first time.

"Sometimes the sun shines so bright that it subdues the moon. But the moon is always there. You just have to take the time to look a little harder. So you see, Coach, nobody can diminish Jemma's light because she *is* light. Her sparkle is always present, even when you choose not to see it. Jules sparkles like no other woman I've ever known."

We lingered in silence for countless heartbeats. I wasn't certain of Quinton's intentions for this meeting. Maybe he wanted to give me some advice. Encourage me not to fumble Jemma, but he was wasting his and my time. I never dropped a ball a day in my life. My record was impeccable, and I did not plan on tainting it.

"Monroe University has been my home for twenty years," Quinton interrupted my inner ponderings. "But it's time for me to go. It'll be best for Shiloh and Jemma. If she is going to love you -"

"If?" I interrupted. Hiking my brows, I was prepared to correct any misconception about me and Jemma.

"I can't watch that," he handed me a piece of paper.

I did not have to view the letter to know that it was his resignation. I looked at him and nodded my head before walking away.

Jules

I gasped a sigh of relief when Ezekiel texted me to let me know he was with his mother. Mrs. Green was the sweetest lady. I was so grateful that God blessed this earth with a little more time with her. She was outspoken, feisty, and brilliant. The doctors were awestruck by her rapid recovery. They'd prepared the family for the worse *if* she woke up, stating they should expect minimal speech, memory loss, and limited mobility. But when Mrs. Green awoke, and they removed the tube, one of the first questions she asked was, '*Why is everybody staring at me like I'm from outer space?*' The room erupted in laughter, including the doctors and nurses.

"Jem, you ready?" Maxine's voice sounded from behind my office door before she walked in.

"Oh, shit. Damn, Jemma," she screeched. "Is this all from Zeke?" Maxi's wide eyes peered around my office in slow motion.

"I wasn't exaggerating when I said he left no surface untouched," I uttered, unable to contain the gleam illuminating my face.

Sitting in my office chair, I swiveled around, following Maxi eyeing the roses and gift boxes.

"Open something," she yelped, clapping her hands together as if it was her birthday.

"Nope. Zeke is going to call me so he can see me open them," I said, much more downcast than I intended.

"Jemma, stop. It's your birthday. You can't be sad on your birthday," Maxi whined, rounding my desk with pouting lips.

She pulled me from my seat and gave me a hug.

"I know, I know. I just wish he was here."

"J, you got it bad."

I nodded, whimpering, "I know."

Maxine and I walked to the quad where the main festivities were taking place. The grills were smoking, the DJ was playing the best old school music, and a plethora of beautiful black brilliant people were fellowshipping. I was overwhelmed almost to tears with birthday well-wishes.

"Happy birthday, Dr. Holiday," the sweetest voice squealed.

I turned around to see my Shiloh. She was dressed in a denim mini skirt and cute ruffle tank top with her box braids bouncing at her waist. My babygirl was steadily improving, and I loved seeing her step into this new phase of her journey.

"Shi. Hi, sweet girl. Thank you," I snuggled into our hug.

"I just came by to say *happy birthday* in person. I'm not trying to hang with the elders."

"Little girl, I am still a tenderoni," Quaron's raspy voice blared from behind me, with Maxi not far behind.

I cackled, then shouted, "Say it again for the people in the back."

"Hi, TT. Hi, Auntie Max," Shiloh greeted her aunts. "I'll leave you *elders* to it," she teased, dodging Quaron's play-fighting.

"Mommy, I'll pick you up tomorrow at noon," Shiloh affirmed, then winked.

I nodded.

"I know Shiloh ain't the good doctor, but you'll still have fun tomorrow. And, we're going to kick it tonight," Quaron uttered, recognizing the momentary shift in my demeanor.

I shook my head, endeavoring to jolt myself out of this periodic funk.

"If you're missing him that much, drop your damn location. That man might hop on the first thing flying out of New York for his Jules," Roni jeered.

"Whatever." I rolled my eyes. "I'm going to get a funnel cake. Do y'all want anything?"

They shook their heads, and I ambled away, ensuring I was out of sight before I looked at my phone. Knowing that it was impossible for Zeke to be here, I dropped my location anyway, just so he would know I was thinking about him.

Immediately, my phone rang, indicating a video call. I smiled, then bit my bottom lip in anticipation of his face on the screen.

"Hey," his baritone muttered.

Zeke's head looked like it was floating in the clouds the way his phone was positioned. But even from that angle, he looked so damn sexy. His sunglasses rested on his bald head, allowing the sunrays to brighten his chocolate eyes.

"Hey," I voiced, barely.

"Happy birthday, baby."

"Thank you."

"You dropped your location."

"I know it's silly. I was just thinking about you."

"I miss you. I hate that I can't be there for your birthday, Jules."

"Your mom is the priority, babe. I understand."

The DJ's speakers thundered as Chrisette Michelle crooned about a couple of forevers.

"I know there are some lovers out there. Where you at?" the DJ yelled, causing the microphone to squeak.

My brow creased in confusion because why would this fool

play slow jams at a staff appreciation barbeque? I circled around, still holding my phone to face the makeshift dance floor. A few couples actually gathered in the middle of the grassy area and cuddled in a slow dance.

I rolled my eyes.

"You good?" Zeke asked, trying to understand why I had a resting bitch face.

"I'm good. My background is loud so I can hardly hear you."

"I actually need to call you back. Give me two minutes," he requested, and I nodded.

I ordered my funnel cake and a lemon slushie, then stepped aside for the other customers. I was still shaking my head as the love song was still playing, and people were still dancing. I was being a hater. The cashier called my name when my phone chimed.

Good Doctor: Location: Monroe City, MO.

The red pin on the map was settled directly in the center of Monroe University. I abandoned the funnel cake, the slushie, every damn thing to find this man. I searched for him through the crowd as if he was a missing child on the playground. My eyes landed on Maxine, Quaron, Shiloh, and Eriya, and finally, my dewy orbs found *him*.

"Zee," I whispered, praying my brain would send a message to my feet not to run.

I attempted to appear composed as I walked in his direction. His smile was all the encouragement I needed to expeditiously get my ass across the grass to get to him. Roni and Maxi stood there gawking like fools while Eriya and Shi smiled warmly, digesting their new normal.

Ezekiel and I glared at each other, indecision and inevitability prancing in our eyes. The background noise was so loud I couldn't decipher if the pounding in my ears was from the music or the symphonic rhythm of my heart beating. The air circulating around us was thick, but his exhales breathed life into my inhales. Our hands fidgeted uncontrollably, eager to connect. The magnetism was potent, and while I did not uncouple my gaze from him, I could sense that the spectators were ready for a show.

"I had to personally wish you happy birthday, Jules," Ezekiel shattered the silence lingering between us.

I extended one hand to palm the curve of his magnificent face. I whispered, "You came." I held my breath, sucking back the ugliest cry.

Zeke imitated my gesture, first stroking a finger down my nose and then arresting my face in his palms.

His forehead lounged against mine as he murmured against my lips, "Every fucking time."

At this point, tears were streaming down my face because I'd been waiting to exhale, and the moment finally arrived when I would allow myself to breathe again. I did not give a damn about who was watching or what private whispers circulated. It didn't matter if I was somebody's wife or somebody's girlfriend. I just yearned to be his forever.

I had the audacity to kiss Dr. Ezekiel Green with an unabashed, brazen fervor in the middle of Monroe University. My body melted into his caress like a dripping ice cream cone on the hottest summer day. Zeke glided his massive hands down my back, resting them right above my ass while swaying to the beat of the music. A *Couple of Forevers* never sounded so good as he clutched me tighter, and I happily surrendered, begging to be held captive by this man.

"Eeww! They're going to be gross, aren't they?" Eriya complained jokingly.

"Yep, pretty much," Shiloh muttered, patting Eriya on the shoulder as they walked away.

Zeke - Later that night

After dinner, Jemma and I rode the elevator to the twenty first floor of The W Hotel. I upgraded our suite a bit from the last time we were in this hotel. Stepping into the room, the roses and gifts from her office had been transported to the hotel suite. She gasped, then turned to gaze at me. Jemma blessed me with the sweetest, most innocent smile. Gratitude and appreciation occupied her eyes.

"Gifts first or a bath?" I asked, recalling that she mentioned soaking in a hot bath.

"Bath," she said to my surprise.

She giggled, seeing the shock on my face. I prepared the jacuzzi tub with a hot bath filled with the sensitive skin bubble bath she used at home. I ushered her into the bathroom, kissing up and down the slope of her neck while removing her clothes. My body was hankering to be one with hers, but I would be patient. She aided me by stripping from her bra and panties, standing before me completely naked. *Damn.* My Jules was a fucking wonder.

We settled in the steamy bath water, pleasantly lingering in silence. Jemma rested against my chest while we basked in the presence of each other.

"Thank you, Ezekiel," she murmured, tracing the outline of my forearm tattoo.

"For what, baby?"

"For allowing me to love you with no shame. Bold and unapologetic. No more thinking, no hesitation, I am coming to you every time, Zee," she promised, then shifted her head to stare up at me.

Jemma's eyes were her soul's narrator. They spoke every unexpressed truth. The wordsmith was often rendered wordless in moments when doubt and unworthiness haunted her. But I was a fucking ghostbuster, ready to rebuke and dispel every falsehood from her subconscious.

Reminiscing on my first encounter with her ex, the same desirous expressions frolicked on my tongue right now. I clenched her face in the curve of my hand.

"Jemma, you are magnificent. A fucking marvel. I love every beautiful flaw, every imperfection. Your scars tell a story of hurt, hope, redemption... freedom. I've spent the last several months digesting every single word, comprehending every fucking paragraph, and I finally understand." I sighed, repositioning her to practically cradle in my arms.

"We'd both been searching to be something to somebody and found each other. The circumstances were not ideal and the journey wasn't smooth, but it is our story, Jules. Our *forever*."

Jemma chuckled, "Our story could make a great book, Dr. Green."

"Oh really. What would you call it? Every fucking time, or, the good doctor Z," I teased, swiping my tongue between her breasts before resting my face on her chest.

"No silly. I would call it... Somebody's Forever."

LOVE NOTE TO MY READERS

Hey Loves! Zeke and Jules have had us in a chokehold for far too long. The friendship and love between these two is undeniable. But what can I say about Dr. Ezekiel Green... ALL MAN! Zeke and Jules will forever be ingrained in my soul.

I don't know what the future holds for Ezekiel and Jemma, but Ezra and Quaron's fiery flame needs to grace the pages.

Follow me on social media to find out! Let me and the world know your thoughts by leaving a review on Amazon or Goodreads.

The Robbi Renee Collection - https://payhip.com/LoveNotesbyRobbiRenee

- French Kiss Duo
- French Kiss Christmas
- French Kiss New Year
- The Pretty Shattered Series
- Pretty Shattered Soul ~ *Available in Audio*
- Pretty Shattered Heart ~ *Available in Audio*

- Pretty Shattered Mind - *Coming Soon*
- Kindred - Xander's Story - ~ *Available in Audio*
- A Beautiful Surprise
- Foreplay
- Somebody's Wife ~ *Available in Audio*

Join my private Facebook Group - Love Notes.

Follow me on Facebook and Instagram, on Twitter @LoveRobbi.

www.lovenotesbyrobbirenee.com

Printed in Great Britain
by Amazon

44445317R00076